# My Mother Never Dies

# My Mother Never Dies

STORIES

*Claire Castillon*

*Translated from the French by*
*Alison Anderson*

Houghton Mifflin Harcourt
*Boston · New York*
2009

Librairie Arthème Fayard, 2006
English translation copyright © 2009 by Alison Anderson
All rights reserved

For information about permission to reproduce selections from this book,
write to Permissions, Houghton Mifflin Harcourt Publishing Company,
6277 Sea Harbor Drive, Orlando, Florida 32887-6777.

www.hmhbooks.com

This is a translation of *Insecte.*

Library of Congress Cataloging-in-Publication Data
Castillon, Claire.
[Insecte. English]
My mother never dies: stories/Claire Castillon;
translated from the French by Alison Anderson.
p. cm.
I. Anderson, Alison. II. Title.
PQ2663.A8249716713 2009 863'.6—dc22
2008011544
ISBN 978-0-15-101426-2

Text set in Fournier MT / Designed by Cathy Riggs

Printed in the United States of America

DOC 10 9 8 7 6 5 4 3 2 1

*For my mother*

# CONTENTS

# My Mother Never Dies

# I Said One

*When* I met my husband, he promised we'd live the good life. We both loved to travel and had, in fact, met in Iran while I was buying a carpet. One simple joke about flying carpets and my husband could later boast to his friends how he seduced me with his sense of humor. We were married at my parents' place—they have an estate in the Touraine— and then moved into a house with a garden. People said it looked like an English cottage. Drinking wine with dinner one evening I shared my greatest phobia with my husband: that a masked man would come into the bedroom through the French doors. My husband put me to bed, promising to have shutters installed, but, of course, the next morning it was all forgotten. I don't tend to worry much, by nature. In fact, men have always appreciated my placid temperament. You can take me anywhere, I adapt to the temperature and the population, I always fit in, find my stride. I'm a real chameleon. We've even lived abroad, going here and there for my husband's job, and, every time, I've found my niche and enjoyed it. New acquaintances, new surroundings, new activities have never cramped my style. On the contrary, I have an optimistic nature, I know how to go for it, it's my credo to make a success of my life. Even after we moved back to France we continued to travel all over the world together because my husband is allowed to take his spouse along on his business trips. I have neither a career nor a dog; I keep myself totally available for him. And, I don't know what your thoughts on the matter might be, but I have my own theories about what a man gets up to when he's alone on a business trip. More than four days on his own, and the wife gets cheated on. Oh, don't make such a face! Have you ever looked into it yourself?

The only territory where I've never been prepared to go along with him, and I'm the first to admit it—I'm not being judgmental, but I do recognize the fact—is in his desire for a child. When he suggested having a baby, it was as if the sky had fallen on my head, I even laughed, I was so sure he must be joking. He didn't mention it again for a while, but it was brewing. He'd dawdle like a schoolgirl outside stores with baby carriages and make this silly grin whenever he saw some sweet little baby doll wiggling in her daddy's arms. Survival instinct or not, I was afraid he might go somewhere else for what he wanted, so, after some negotiating, I agreed to become a mother. I warned him that I would only have one. He looked stunned, but that was the way it had to be, I was agreeing to it out of my love for him, and on the condition we have a daughter. Sooner or later I'd probably grow attached to her, otherwise she'd have to make do with distant affection. My husband was over the moon. I got pregnant very quickly; he treated me like a queen even before my stomach began to swell. I was completely spoiled and I even got a necklace. It was one of those, what do they call them, diamond *rivières*, I think, though the diamonds were fake, of course, there was no way he'd give me real ones, but this looked just as good! I remember one dinner party where the women trooped over to my table to admire my gorgeous necklace. And no, I didn't admit that it was fake, it was none of their business.

So where was I? Oh yes, pregnant. What a fuss! My stomach blew up all at once, I was on the verge of despair, after almost forty years of my life spent standing up straight so that I wouldn't slouch like my fellow creatures. They ran some routine tests, and that's when they realized I was expecting twins. I asked right away whether they were Siamese; the idea of having two children joined at the shoulder or the foot or the spleen really disgusted me. Good looking as we are, my husband and I, I can't see us carrying such a burden. And he's not much of a handyman, so it wouldn't exactly be a piece of cake for him to retrofit a baby carriage or a bed with the right dimensions. It was while I was thinking about all these little everyday things that I suggested—and perhaps I might have been a bit abrupt—getting rid of one of them. The doctor assured me that there was no possible comparison between Siamese twins and regular twins. For some reason he looked appalled while he was explaining the difference.

Children aren't exactly a specialty of mine, but they nearly became so. Can you imagine? A woman nearly forty wakes up one day to find herself having to put up with two screaming brats? Even my husband, who has the reputation of a saint, baptized them the bed wetters. I don't mean to tattle on anyone, but I would like to point out that the miserable rat is not beyond reproach in this business.

Two daughters, what a mess! And what a fright just imagining the mischief they'd get into as teenagers! But they were growing nicely. People would look at them in the street and ask all sorts of idiotic questions to which I'd give any old answer. I wasn't about to tell them what order the girls had been born in or if I'd been in much pain: I didn't have the faintest idea—I was asleep. And then it took me forever to learn how to tell them apart. At last I found a nifty trick thanks to the little callus on the thumb each one sucked. One sucked her right thumb and the other sucked her left one, and the one who sucked her right thumb had the letter $R$ in her name. Enough about their infancy. As you can see, two kids was a lot to deal with.

When they turned three it was time to take them to school for the first time. Up until then we'd always used my husband's sedan, but he chose the perfect day to be away on business. Honestly! So I'm the one who got the girls ready. They'd been up for six hours, overexcited at the idea of wearing their little backpacks for the first time. They'd swapped their dresses and were squabbling over some little barrette, so I had no choice but to break it in two. Of course then they began to cry, refused to have breakfast or put their jackets on or walk out to the car. I struggled with the $R$ one, she was clinging to the sofa cushions—so I had to carry her. And me with my bad back. Then, one thing after another, of course they wouldn't fit right in my smart car. I tried to squeeze one of them into the trunk but it was full from the strollers. Finally, I just sat one on top of the other in the passenger's seat and got on the road. They were screaming as loud as could be, so I couldn't hear a thing on the radio. Great way to start the day. I opened the car door and I threw the one on top out onto the beltway. And to be honest, I wasn't very pleased with what I'd done because I threw out the better behaved of the two.

Let me make one thing clear: I warned my husband. I didn't play any underhanded tricks. I did say yes, but I said one.

# The Insect

*He* waits for her in the corridor, eagerly anticipates her bath, while I get dinner ready. This has been going on for two or three weeks, since he had a funny reaction when he saw her little bra drying among the laundry on the rack above the bathtub. He asked me why she was wearing one now, and I explained that it was a good idea for her to start early, to get used to wearing one as quickly as possible, the minute her breasts began to bud. He stood there touching the straps, the cups, gently, and then opened the medicine cabinet and took out a stick of deodorant and said he'd give it to her so that he could be part of her little transformation, too. I explained that this was the sort of thing that women normally deal with among themselves, so he didn't insist, just handed me the stick, and I'm the one who initiated our daughter into the use of deodorant. But unfortunately whatever was eating at him didn't go away. At dinner I could see he was staring at her and at her bra—you could sort of see it through the sweater she'd borrowed from me. But after that I didn't notice anything else until one evening I found him next to the bathroom sink sniffing our little girl's towel. I saw him clearly, but figured he must have just taken the wrong towel, but I said something all the same, made a point about principles of hygiene. I wasn't expecting him to apologize, but he said he was sorry and put the towel back on the rack. He had just been wiping his face, that was all.

Except that our little girl is starting to behave strangely, too. In the evening she often hides in the kitchen while I'm mending things or making meals ahead of time that I dish out into plastic containers and freeze. She wants to sit next to me, reading or learning how to sew. She doesn't seem to enjoy as much going down to the garage with her father, where he's made a little niche where he can be free to tinker around, right below the ground floor. And lately he's taken a dislike to it if I show up there without an invitation, but it's different for our little girl when she spends time with him, watching him work or put things away or paint. When I go down there I don't venture too far, not that he'd yell or any-thing but I know it's his territory. It's like my kitchen—we each have our secret garden, so I stand there on the thresh-old and just tell our little girl it's time for bed.

My husband set up a buzzer between the garage and the kitchen, so when he needs something he buzzes once for our little girl to go downstairs, twice for me. If we're avail-able, of course. Otherwise he comes upstairs, and he doesn't grumble, it's not like he's holding us hostage or anything. Sometimes he just feels like having a snack or looking at a book or a newspaper. He gets the inspiration for his paint-ings from pictures he finds here and there. And he's actually very talented.

When he comes up from the garage—where he's been since after dinner, fiddling around for hours on end—it is well past midnight and often I'm already in bed, so he slides quietly in between the sheets. But lately he's been going to see her in her bedroom first; I can hear him go in and close the door behind him. So I close my eyes. I saw a program on TV about incest, and I explained the word to our little girl. She didn't know it and she gave a sort of naive laugh. That re-assured me. But then I suspect my husband doesn't use the word with her when he does it. I put my hands on my ears;

I'd prefer not to hear what they're up to, it would be too up-setting, like seeing it happen. Since my mother died, I can't stand any kind of strong feelings, it makes my head spin, sometimes it even puts me right to sleep. On Wednesday our little girl fell down and just seeing the blood on her knees made me feel all strange. I didn't know what to do to take care of her and I had to call her father. I wanted to go down to the garage to get him but my daughter wouldn't let me, she said she'd rather go on her own, as if he had threatened her. She took the disinfectant and the gauze strips, and I handed her the scissors, the long ones, the ones that cut really well. Once her knee was bandaged she came back up and helped me in the kitchen. I stroked the top of her head, trying to wash something away, and then she cut her finger on the lid of a can. The blood was spurting out and she started crying, so I scolded her, then I started crying, too. I pressed the buzzer for my husband to come up and help us. I was trying not to blink, not to miss a thing, a single gesture. I saw him take our little girl's finger, clean it and bandage it. I didn't notice anything particular between them, scarcely a ripple of feeling even though she was still bleeding and at one point it even dripped on to her little-girl thighs. Then my husband went back downstairs to work and suggested our little girl go with him, but she refused. She looked at me and said she wanted to stay and help me. To lighten the mood, I told her she should sit down somewhere and just watch, because otherwise she'd never make it to the end of the day. So we started laughing, all three of us, like before, and I felt a deep flutter of well-being moving inside me. For a moment I was afraid that it meant another child, and why not a girl, or an insect. That's what I thought, in that order. A poisonous insect that would drive my husband crazy all over again a few years down the road. Our daughter is becoming so graceful, I don't want him to crush her. But how can I confront him without ruining everything? We have it so good here together, we can't change a thing.

My daughter comes to kiss me good night. We are sitting in the living room, and we look at my collection of miniature insects laid out on the table. She strokes the blue beetle dangling from the chain around my neck, gives it little nicknames. She's known this beetle since she was born. My husband has always encouraged me to collect these little creatures, he says that I'm a strange little creature myself, a weird insect, an odd woman. Our little girl is allowed to touch the beetles only in my presence—you can break them by just looking at them so you have to know exactly how to go about it. Like men, they look strong, with their carapace, armor, antennae. I wonder if as soon as night falls they're all headed off to scratch at my daughter's door, and the most agile among them will slip under it, to take her. Master's orders. But I shouldn't go imagining such scenes. I have to protect myself, stifle the feeling that overwhelms me the moment he goes into her room.

Besides, my husband was quick this evening—he's already leaving our little girl's room. He comes in and lies down beside me and says, "Good evening, Gorgeous," kissing me on the mouth. I detect my daughter's scent and hold him against me as if I were holding her in her bed, ravaged by the man who is now in mine. I put my hand on his sex, I want to see how long it is, exactly the length that went inside my daughter. This arouses him again. He takes me—like her? How does he take her? The young girl is taking my place. My husband is making love to me, whispering crude things in my ear, sometimes his words are frenzied but gentle, too, loving. To make me come he says, There, there—the way you calm a child.

One night, our little girl cries out and my husband jumps out of bed, rushes into her room. I get up, too, carried by a force, yes this time I really do feel strong, I go to the door that he has closed carefully behind him. I listen and all I can hear is a daddy saying, "There, there." He has to calm the child, otherwise how can he explain to her that he has no right to be doing what he is doing, even if he is doing it quite decently, without any improper thoughts. I hurry back to bed and he follows soon afterward, it was just a nightmare, everything is fine now. Tomorrow she'll be at school, she'll be safe. Later, tomorrow maybe, I'll find the courage and take her away, far from here, far from him. I stick close to my husband; I love this man so much, his skin and his smell, his presence and his voice. This is all my fault. I should never have bought a bra for my daughter so early. What sort of perverse need did I have, talking about her little budding breasts to a man, a man who lives under the same roof? Am I out of my mind?

In the morning they leave for school, he drops her off, it's on his way. She is allowed to sit in front, now that she wears a bra. She waves to me, smiling from behind the glass; she forgives me for abandoning her to her torturer, it's classic. That's what they said, on the TV show. A child who is abused by her father will defend her mother. By complying with what is asked of her, she ensures the equilibrium of the family. Or something like that. This morning, her father was winking at her. I pretended not to notice but when he said,

"See you down in the garage, I'm taking the car out," he winked. I wanted to go down with her, to be there, to see what was going on, but she stopped me. She said, "It's bad enough my father takes me to school, I don't need my mother to take me down to the garage," and shrugged her shoulders. I didn't want to insist, I could tell she was protecting me and that it would be disingenuous of me to question her consideration.

While she's at school I wash her laundry and her towels, figuring that if my husband might get excited by a smell—they always talk about pheromones where sex is concerned—I'd better wash everything. The little flying insect dangles round my neck and bounces between my breasts while I'm hard at work getting everything spic and span. Everything has to smell clean. I don't want him to touch her anymore. I don't want him to leave.

This evening I'm sitting in the kitchen waiting for my husband and my daughter; she has laid the table and it looks lovely, ready for a celebration—it's my birthday. And suddenly I hear the buzzer. One buzz. My daughter runs down to the garage. I let her go. It's my birthday. In twenty minutes the roast will be ready, they have just enough time to feel each other up a bit before dinner. She didn't look anxious when she left to go down, maybe she likes it after all, maybe there are some civilizations where it's a common practice, it's a question of culture. I wait in the kitchen, trying not to think about anything. I concentrate on the shape of my organs. And suddenly the buzzer is ringing nonstop, not just once or twice but a regular wailing siren, as if my daughter's body were pressed against the wall, against the buzzer with no reprieve as if, crushed by her father, she can no longer spare her mother. Her cry penetrates the kitchen walls while the roast is oozing and the potatoes are turning golden next to the cooking meat. And the buzzer rings like crazy. I run down the stairs, listen at the door and hear my husband say that they'll never manage to get it up. He says, "get it up." At this point, what have I got to lose: I open the garage door. If it is too terrible to see I'll close it again gently and everything will be just as before. I see my husband at one end of the room and my little girl at the other, her back against the wall, and my husband is grumbling as he stands there by the workbench. Their hands are gripping a huge rectangle that they're trying to move, cautiously, so that they don't damage it. My daughter sees me and says— No need to take it up the back stairs, we can go in through the front door. Look who's here! My husband puts the object down, and the sheet that was covering it slips to one side,

revealing a painting—measuring twelve by six—the por-
trait of a woman who looks like an insect, a beetle for my
birthday.

My daughter is eating her roast. She says they had the hard-
est time hiding the painting all this time, for a month she's
been following his progress day by day, it was her idea for
the drawing, even if her father was the one who did the
painting. What they really wanted was to see the surprise
on my face, had I really not noticed anything? Nothing se-
cretive in their behavior? They were afraid that all their
conspiring might make me feel rejected. They wanted the
painting to be gigantic, like their love for me. I am crying.
My daughter is smiling. Then my man holds me against him,
tight, and says, "There, there," and I ask him if he wants
any more potatoes, they're Touquet, fairly rare, but I still
managed to find some.

# A Parka and
# Some Fur-lined Boots

"*Come on*! You're the one who wanted to go out and now you're taking forever. There won't be anything left! I'm warning you, if the leather jackets are all gone, I'll be pissed. It's just like last time, when we got there after everyone else, thanks to you. What's the point of going to the sales if that's the way it's going to be? You might as well just give me the money and let me go alone. And I don't understand why you're glued to me like this, anyway, I'm old enough to go shopping by myself. All you're interested in is studying the labels to see if something's going to lose its shape or if it's washable and in the meantime all the good stuff vanishes. Come *on*, all you have to do is put one foot in front of the other, of course if you try to put both feet forward at the same time you won't get anywhere—are you doing this on purpose or what?"

She has no idea how much she irritates me with her cancer. They prescribed a tiny bout of radiation to start off with, it couldn't have been that bad. Nine sessions of chemotherapy. As Dad would say, she made such a big deal out of it that she let the disease take over. As a result she doesn't have a single hair left on her head and her wig itches, so she takes it off a lot. We told her we were kind of shocked she did that because her bald head is embarrassing, but she takes the wig off all the same. For a laugh we call her Egghead or Yul Brynner or Billiard Ball. Makeup doesn't cover her yellowed complexion anymore but she's really stubborn so she keeps putting on way too much, and the other day when I was walking with her out in the garden at the hospital I heard someone say, "Here comes the drag queen," so to make a joke out of it I told her she ought to get herself hired at a cabaret. But it didn't make her laugh, and I had to explain to her that it was supposed to be funny. Jeez, lighten up, already.

She walks really slowly, she breathes like an ox, I think she's been drinking, when she speaks I can only get half of what she says, and she's bleary eyed. So I try to be home as little as possible when she's there; after class I hang around in the café, and on weekends I go and stay with friends.

"Come *on*," I said, "there's stuff at 50 percent off but by the time we get there it will be only the stuff at 20 percent off that's left, and then there's no point, we'll have come all this way for nothing. Move it, for Chrissakes. And hide your oozy stomach bag, it's sticking out."

She grabs my arm, which exasperates me and makes me feel like I'm walking my grandmother. I'm going to buy her a leash with a harness, give her something to really suffocate about. At least she picks up speed a little bit. I adjust the collar of her coat and she thanks me, which annoys me. Time to stop all these thank yous and sighs and sappy behavior. She asks me to calm down, even though I am calm, I just want to get the jacket, the black one, the one my friend has. Mom says that if there aren't any in this store we'll look somewhere else, even at the regular price, in any case she wants to give it to me, she promised, so I tell her that we really can't be throwing money out the window like that. It's not like they put these sales on for no reason, or like they're just throwing the merchandise out for the dogs. And you know what? I want a dog. By the way I got an F in physics but I don't care because I'm going to go for a literary diploma.

And I got thrown out of gym class because I was smoking in the locker room, but maybe you'd like to lecture me about tobacco? Go right ahead, that would be a good laugh.

In the store everyone stares at her, she looks like one of those pictures in the history books, nothing but bones beneath her skin, her face drained away by the devil, as the history teacher says. As a result we get served first, someone offers her a chair, and I tell them it's okay. For two minutes she can stand up. She says the jacket is pretty, hands me cardigans and thick sweaters with big collars, and coats, and scarves, asks if they have bonnets, says I need to keep warm this winter. They ask her to repeat what she said. Speak clearly! They can't understand you, there are sales on, don't you get it? The salespeople have better things to do than to try to read your lips, so make an effort! She finds a parka for me with a fur-lined hood and big pockets, she says it's good to have pockets, that way you can put everything in them and travel light. I tell her I'm not about to travel anywhere, so she insists, You can lend it to me, go ahead and get it.

She really annoys me with all her comments. My girlfriend's mother, when she had her cancer, she didn't make a big deal out of it, and now she's cured. She went on living as if there were nothing wrong. Maybe it hadn't spread, but she made an effort, and willpower is the key to success, that's all there is to it. Whereas if you only think about yourself . . . what can you expect? If my mother thought about us once in a while, if she thought about me, she wouldn't let herself fall so low, no way, there's something sadistic about the way she imposes her disease on us, like she's passing it on to us. Come on, let's get out of here, people have stared at us long enough. I want to go home. And I hate it when Mom spoils me, anyway, it makes me want to cry. Even when she wasn't sick I didn't like it, it gave me the feeling that I'd had to share a part of my day with her and that I'd taken advantage of her in some way, and all that was in it for her was a bit of relaxation and oblivion. But she doesn't want to go home, she really wants to buy me some leather boots for around town, and also some fur-lined boots. I tell her we'll see once winter is here, but she thinks it's a good idea to buy them now. While I'm trying on a pair I like, she puts on some boots she feels comfortable in, she says they're very warm and comfy, so the saleswoman exclaims, I don't know how you can try those on in this heat! What an idiot that woman was! What business is it of hers? My mother rolls her eyes and buys a pair, and says she'll wear them home, and we leave the store.

She asks me if she can take her wig off, the heat is making her head swell up but she'll put on a scarf. She hides as best she can behind a tree and replaces her fake hair with a poorly knotted turban.

"You tied it on all crooked. You look like a madwoman."

"Can you fix it for me, please?"

"If I help you, then take off your fur-lined boots. I don't want people staring at us."

It's as if she doesn't hear, but, as Dad said, cancer doesn't make you deaf, at least not the kind she has, so this just proves she's turning a deaf ear. She sent her head on vacation and left us to deal with her disgusting body. I'm the one who had to wash her legs again last night. She called me from the bathtub, she couldn't move them any more.

She wants to stop for a snack at four o'clock, we have to eat. I agree on condition that she eats some cake, too, but she feels nauseated, and I tell her to stop focusing on all her aches and pains. She tells me to leave her alone, just until she's gone. She says it for me, says she's going to die, and before too long. She says, "Listen to me. Even if it's hard to accept, I'm going to die and I'm nearly there." I laugh, a sort of pretend laugh, the way my father does, he has tears in his eyes a lot lately, like my brother who looks down at his feet and whose voice just won't stop changing, one minute up then down, paradise or hell, the choice is his, he isn't sure, I guess he's been afraid for a long time, like me.

I'm crying, loud painful sobs. If my mother weren't here, who would tell me things so simply, just like this? She's the one person I can believe when she says she's going to die. Not the doctors who promised they'd save her. We sit down on a bench. I pull on my fur-lined boots, my sweater, and my parka. Next winter will be a tough one but for the time being I've still got her warmth to stock up on. I let her slip her frozen hand into my pocket. On we go. Homeward, we're nearly there. It's like our heart: other end of the main artery, first on the left.

# My Best Friend

*My* daughter is my best friend. We've always been good companions; always understood each other; and feel drawn to each other in a natural, light-hearted way. Since she turned fourteen we've even been talking about sex. I tell her how to dress to be attractive; how to prepare her body for lovemaking; how to rub, caress, seduce. When we're out in the street we have fun just looking at men, and when they turn to look at us, sometimes we burst out laughing, sticking our tongues out at them. We really are compatible. I always say that she is very lucky to have experienced, over and above the bond with her father, this symbiosis that is intensely close and unconstrained by authority or rules. She calls me by my first name, I go with her to discos, and teach her friends how to make tequila slammers. In the meantime her father waits for me at home and occasionally complains about my so-called teenage crisis. He is responsible and serious; I trust him with the shopping and the housekeeping. When he comes home from work he finds both of us in Cathy's room; we're trying to solve the world's problems. Sitting on her bed, we talk about Jérôme, the boy she likes, and Lorie, her favorite singer. We put movie posters on the wall, take fashion photos, put on makeup, dance to music at full blast, and fly into his arms when he comes into the room. He sets the table while we finish playing. I keep some frozen meals on hand that we can heat up quickly for dinner. Sometimes I send my husband out to get McDonald's, and when there are toys in the Happy Meal, we throw them at him. We like the way he looks at times like this.

During dinner Cathy and I tell her father what's going on at school. Sometimes he tells me to let her speak, apparently I make too much of a deal out of her news. Cathy and I burst out laughing. And while she tells him about school we give each other little kicks under the table, the way Jérôme did at the disco the other night when he was trying to play footsie with her and went for me instead! If my husband thinks we're being too childish, he tells us we're pests and asks us to help him clear the table, and we give in, especially Cathy, who doesn't like to displease him. But there's no way we'll give in about choosing what to watch on TV. We have no problem clicking away from his news program to that game with the newlyweds who compete trying to figure out what the other person wants. Lately it's been kind of hard for me to see her going off to bed all alone, when we could have gone on being girls and blabbing half the night away, but I also have to remember that I have a husband and, contrary to what he sometimes claims, when I'm negotiating the terms of our outings to nightclubs I am careful to fulfill my duties as a wife at the same time. Just because I know how to have a really good time doesn't mean I'm no longer kittenish and affectionate with my husband. Anyway, playing the good wife is one way to show my daughter how to keep a man.

Well, naturally my husband has a tendency to make me pay for my high spirits at dinner, so when he's hurt and annoyed because we've been huddling together muttering our secrets, his restraint is equal to whatever I have withheld in the way of attention. Moreover, on this particular evening, while I've been rubbing up against him, plotting what might be the best strategy to stop Véro, Cathy's enemy, from going after Jérôme, my husband tells me that my schoolgirl outfit doesn't turn him on in the least, and asks me to try to dress the way I used to. I get angry; he can't stand to see me having fun. I lie on top of him and reassert my rights, but he turns his head to one side and says that, frankly, he has no desire either to see or to fuck my Mickey Mouse nightie. And he says it in just that way, using just that verb. I suggest he try ripping it off me and he looks at me, horrified. Incredulous, I sit on the edge of the bed.

"You are really, like, so wack."

"I beg your pardon?"

"Wack, bro. You don't know shit."

"Have you gone out of your mind? Can you hear the way you're talking? You ought to be teaching Cathy how to mind her language a bit more. Have you even seen her grades in French? But instead you give her biology lessons, just in case she can't figure out all by herself where to put it in and how it works! Have you completely lost your mind?"

"Go fuck yourself."

I burst out laughing, jump up, and hurry to Cathy's bedroom. I see that she's asleep and I put the light on low to ask her if I can sleep in her bed. She's sort of groggy but she lifts the sheets for me to join her. We spend the night together and there between us, etched on our chests, are

Mickey Mouse the tennis champ for her and Mickey Mouse the jazz buff for me.

The next morning the mood is glum. My husband, all dressed and ready to go to work, kisses Cathy; nothing for me. So I burst out laughing. He gives me such a dark look that I have to cringe to contain myself, and he goes out, slamming the door. Cathy and I wait a few seconds, then explode with laughter. Afterward she tells me she doesn't like it when I fight with her papa. Tomorrow, Saturday, we'll go shopping and maybe do a bit of bowling, but only if it rains, otherwise we'd rather hang around the garden, go Rollerblading, that's cool. My husband—and I don't want to call him Jean-Jacques, that sounds too uncool, let's call him Jacky—has shown up on the other side of the fence with the shopping. I rush over to grab a package of cookies from him and hand them out to everyone. Sometimes I complain because he buys those Paille d'or things and honestly, you have to do better if you want to make an impression on the gang. But Cathy says I ought to stop dissing her father like this all the time.

I've given my daughter a cell phone on the sly. Her father was against the idea, he couldn't see the point for a teenager who will just use up her minutes every evening repeating to her friends the same things she'd already told them in detail, and then some, all day long. But since we really wanted to be able to stay in touch, at least by texting, I bought her a little tiny one that she switches off as soon as her dad gets home. If she's talking, I clear my throat or say very loudly, Oh darling, is that you? Home already?

When I'm at the office I'm amazed to hear how my colleagues talk about their children as if they were some sort of virus or societal problem. When I join in these conversations, when I show them my vacation or weekend photos, I can see that some of them envy me, but others are shocked, they say the same things my husband does, bringing up all the business about borders and limits. But my daughter is not some sort of enemy territory.

My husband, however, has not recovered from my insult last night. And his mood is no better this evening than this morning. I retreat to my daughter's room and we put our heads together and finally come up with the way to get rid of Véro, who is the only obstacle preventing Jérôme from yielding at last to Cathy's advances. We have managed to take a photo of Véro hanging on to some boy at a nightclub, even though she's said she loves Jérôme and promised she'd never let any other boy kiss her. She can just forget it now! I tell the story to my husband, who replies that, frankly, he doesn't see what business it is of mine. Things are still strained between us, we sleep facing opposite directions, we wake up and get up and never even touch hands, he closes the bathroom door, spreads butter on his bread, only cuts enough bread for himself and Cathy. He fixes his coffee, does his laundry, buys his food, drinks his wine, keeps his things separate from mine, but so what, I've got Cathy, my best friend. Sometimes I can sense she's ill at ease, she wonders if her father isn't right to feel hurt by our complicity and whether I shouldn't try to get closer to him and play my role as a woman—be his woman, I should say. A woman isn't a role. I try to get her to come down off her high horse a bit, but she stays right up there. This is her new way of reasoning, she says a mother isn't an adolescent. I know she'll get over it so I go off to bed, lie down next to my husband, humming this great new hit, while he reads a book about rural life in France. Fortunately tomorrow evening Jérôme is coming for dinner, we'll have fun.

I'm making a casual dinner, and my husband pouts when he sees the potato chips and club sandwiches. I look to Cathy for support, but her cold glare goes right through me; discreetly, she tells me I should have come up with something else, because we aren't going to make much of an impression on Jérôme, when you remember his father runs a gourmet country inn. And great idea to have salad that will stick between our teeth. I try to make them laugh by imitating the way the math teacher lisps, but when Jérôme is surprised at how well informed I am, Cathy just says, Forget it, she doesn't know her. My husband devours his club sandwich, his chips, and his glass of red wine, keeping a pathetic smile on his face.

After dinner I stay behind with him for a while—well, in the same room, that is, because he's busy. Nobody cleared the table, Cathy shut herself in her room with Jérôme. I figure I'll go spend some time with them, we could dance to the music from our Destroy-Enigma compilation, I go and get it from the car. When I come back up I knock on the door to Cathy's room and go in. I find her sitting astride Jérôme, so I go back out quietly and grab the camera from the drawer in the kitchen, and then go back into her room. They are so absorbed by their kissing that they don't hear me come in and, Snap! you lovebirds, I've got your photo. What the hell are you doing, shouts my daughter, are you out of your mind? She grabs the camera and throws it on the floor, points her finger at me, and says, You are going to leave me alone, you hear? You're a leech! You have no business here. What you're doing is just ugly, it's wrong, you're sick in the head, completely whacked! She shoves me out of the room, pushing me back with one hand on each breast, then slams the door in my face.

My husband, curious to see what the fuss is about, finds me sitting on the floor, in a state of shock, holding the CD set against my chest. He continues on his way, and all he says is, Are you coming to bed?

I know things will be better tomorrow, I have faith. They say it's perfectly normal, these kinds of violent confrontations between girlfriends in their teens.

# They Drank Champagne
# at the Restaurant

*I have* supraventricular tachycardia. My heart often goes into panics, but my mother says this will pass. With age, your emotions fade. For the time being, it's enough to identify the source of my fear and avoid it in time. My heart starts beating fit to burst whenever he says, Well, actually, and I feel like I'm about to get the same awful jolt as when he says, Oh, now that I think about it, or, By the way, I think I forgot to mention. I wish I were deaf, so what I see with my own eyes could not be misrepresented by my husband. What I don't want is to be told fibs, because my pretending not to notice all this makes me complicit with the fib and, deep inside, my heart knows I have betrayed it and it is beside itself with pounding. My heart is much more spontaneous than I am about these things. It might fail me. It takes off even before the lie is uttered, but my husband can't hear it beating, so he says these things anyway. Live and let live, says Mother, he's not doing any harm, he puts in a lot of hours, don't go looking for some mystery, you took him on with the defects of his qualities, he's hard working, you won't change him, you have to accept people the way they are. He probably has things he'd reproach you with, she went on, things to say about you and your behavior, the way you don't keep your commitments. Besides, what makes you think he's lying? If you worked you'd know that a meeting is something that truly does exist.

I'm tachycardiac and paranoid. Leave him alone, says my mother again, he might get mad, and he'd be absolutely in the right.

So I let things go, let my heart quietly panic when he informs me that he'll be coming home later than planned, or when he calls me, already out for the evening, far away, to say, Hey, listen, I'm not sure I told you. So then I call my mother, I'd really like some company if my heart is going to race, even if I don't talk about it, just time enough for it to calm down, time enough to talk about something else, but my mother often lets her answering machine pick up.

And so, to pass the time, I rummage through his letters and photos. I'm looking for dates, symbols, messages, there's one box I've never opened, I didn't see the point in going through his clothes trunk when there are already so many clues in every corner of his study, in his shoe boxes. I've discovered that he went out with Céline Demongin des Gachons at college, although when I ask him about it he assures me he didn't. He says he doesn't like her style or her ideas and he's never been unfaithful to me. If it happened back in college he would tell me, now that we're married. But in the letters I found she writes words like *my love, my body again,* and I don't know what else, *hot from your skin, your dead sex,* something I can't decipher, *with my fingers, our lips mingled.*

I leave a message on Mother's answering machine, I tell her that Patrice did indeed have an affair with Céline Demongin des Gachons. Remember? The girl with the leather jacket, oh, come on, you know, the one who had an eye operation, it doesn't matter, call me back if you think it does, I'd like to talk about it for a while, not even a long while. I know I'm annoying you. I didn't really search, I could have come across that stuff by chance, but what do you think she means by dead sex?

———

Waiting for my mother to call me back I feel my heart gallop as I turn through the pages of our wedding album, telling myself that I ought to be happy that it's been five years today, will he remember when he comes home later? He forgot our four-year anniversary, but Mother told me just to drop it, it's typical of people who don't do a thing all day to obsess about dates for stupid reasons. I might have some really good news to announce tonight, but I don't know yet how I'll go about it. Mother tells me not to overdo it, you can only really be sure after three months have gone by. If I'm pregnant, that will move my heart to my belly: The heart beating fast, inside me, will be the child's, and I won't need to go drawing on the strength of my own heart anymore to invent the beating, it will be there, really there, this other heart, strong, beating inside me.

I call Mother to find out if she'd like to come with me to the pharmacy to buy my pregnancy test. I think that this time I'm not getting carried away, it seems possible. I'm very tired, they say that's how it starts, right? Are you there? Call me when you get back in, I'll wait a little while before I go out, I'd prefer to go with you.

Heart racing some more. I mustn't think about it. But it's from that blue slip of paper, from the restaurant receipt with the champagne. A lunch date. On a Wednesday. At the Auberge du Cheval Blanc. On a day when he was on a business trip to Angers with the regional director. He came home at ten that night, but I didn't say anything, so as not to annoy him. I just called Mother to calm myself down. Anyway, she couldn't answer, she was out with a girlfriend. When I went to wash my husband's trousers there was an unbearable little streak on his fly, like a thin little glue, as if a girl had been sitting on him, there, I've said it. The receipt was in his pocket. I try Mother again. This time I really need to speak to you, I say, I'm trying everything not to, but nothing's working, I feel like going over there, to his office, I have to see him, he's seeing someone, they've been drinking champagne. Forgive me, but I'm losing it, come right away, I'm in a major panic.

I reread the receipt, I call the restaurant, they can't remember my husband, so as for whoever was with him, to be honest . . . and besides it wasn't just yesterday.

"People who drink champagne at lunchtime, do you get a lot of those?" I say to the restaurant owner.

"To celebrate an event, sometimes, or two lovers."

"If I drop by and show you a photo of my husband, would you remember if there was a woman with him?"

"You can always try. I'll tell you if I do."

"Because I might be pregnant, you understand?"

"Come if you'd like."

"And if I am pregnant, you have to tell me all the same, don't spare me."

"It's all the same to me, I don't know you."

"Obviously. He's not drinking his champagne with me."

"So come have a little glass, it will help you relax!"

So I call Mother again, because the fear is there, in my stomach, and maybe with two arms and two legs it will have what it takes to grab hold of me now. Mother, you've got to call me back, even if I annoyed you with Cécile Demongin des Gachons, I'm sorry, let it go, it's not about her anymore, he's been drinking champagne at a restaurant, I tell you. I don't know if I should call his office to find out if he was in Angers the day of the receipt from the restaurant in Paris, but I can't go on being blind. Do you think a restaurant in Angers could have an address in Paris? It happens sometimes with restaurant chains, doesn't it? Or maybe it's the address of the headquarters, but do restaurants have headquarters? My head is spinning, Mother, I took the pill you told me to take, but I didn't think about what if I'm pregnant. I'm going to walk over to the pharmacy, you can meet me there directly. If the test is positive, I might have to have my stomach pumped, I'll confess to the pharmacist that I took a little pill you told me to take for tachycardia, even if it's no great sin, right? I feel so sleepy, like I can't help it— what's that called again?

But my heart is racing all the same, even though I feel dazed, and sleepy, and it's so complicated to cross the street. So I stand there by the light—green, red, green. I try to act natural, I won't disturb anyone, just standing in the middle of the boulevard since I didn't manage to cross it in one go. Traffic in both directions, on either side of me, like the blood in my arteries, I can feel it going through me, that blood, pounding like a locomotive. I take advantage of another pedestrian crossing over the second stretch, I close my eyes, go nearer to him and, when he sets off, his movement leads me. Only a hundred yards left to the pharmacy. My husband is so squeamish about all that stuff, it's up to me to count the days. Besides, he doesn't like doing it with me very much, with the others he drinks champagne, to me he says he's scared of how fragile I am, all that. The evenings when we decide to come together, I do a headstand afterward in secret in the bathroom, so that the baby will take good hold.

————

I pull out my cell phone. Mother gave it to me so I can reach her under any circumstances, in case I have a little panic attack in the street. She always says so little, you can tell she's not the one having an attack.

Mother, I'm here, I'm in the street, I'm trying not to think about the receipt from the restaurant, but it's complicated all the same, people are staring at me, and I'm so sleepy, I don't know if I'm going to make it to the pharmacy. Just in case, if anything happens, for the time being I'm just outside number thirteen on the boulevard, oh gosh, thirteen, do you suppose that's a sign?

My body feels like lead as I go by number thirteen, I have to force myself, push a weight forward with each foot. And what if I called *him*, why don't I ever tell *him* when things aren't right, after all? I don't dare, it's really weird when you think, I'm his wife, what does it matter if I call him, huh Mother, if it's for something exceptional, because my heart is beating too fast? He never wants to touch my heart, because it's under my breast, I suppose, but my husband should like touching my breast, no? Mother, are you there? Shall I call him or not?

Outside the pharmacy I call my husband. I like his voice on the answering machine, it reminds me of the voice he has

when he speaks to other people. When he speaks to them he
has a very warm, soft voice, out of respect, no doubt, whereas
with me he speaks in spurts, a bit forced, it's due to shyness,
it's hard to find the right tone to speak to your wife. So to his
machine I say that I'm calling to congratulate him on his
voice and that he ought to try to use the same one with me,
especially as now we are going to be parents, that will bring
us closer, and just then I hang up, my heart is racing, what
do I know, I'm not sure of anything and already I'm telling
him? I go into the pharmacy, buy a pregnancy test, go back
out and rush over to his office. I go into the building, up to
the seventh floor, I know that's where it is, my husband always says that to stay in shape he climbs his six flights from
the ground floor every day. I open a door, a young woman at
reception tries to stop me from going past, so I give her a
shove, she falls over, and I head along the hallway, and the
walls are leaning like on the day I had my allergic reaction to
codeine in some cough syrup Mother had given me. There's
my name on one of the doors. With his first name. And in I
go, without knocking, I should be at home here.

And that's when I see Mother with her legs spread, her
ass on the desk, and him with his fingers inside, his tongue
hanging out of his mouth, his face buried in her neck. My
heart's not racing anymore, no, my heart comes to a complete

stop. Both of them look up. He keeps his fingers inside of her and Mother, her mouth open and her face all pink, in shock, continues jerking off my husband.

I turn around, into the hallway, and go down the stairs. I have to get across the boulevard, go home, pack a suitcase, leave, see the lawyer, divorce, and live far away, under another identity. Maybe on an island. Run a sailing club or open a school. Or maybe an infirmary. But I'm afraid of shots. I've heard that in Besançon you can— Or maybe the mountains. I'll go by train. And I'll rent a car. I already have my learner's permit, I just don't have the license. I'll take a cab. Or hitchhike. Hitchhiking is good. But first, just one thing to do, find out how far along—

In the middle of the boulevard, against the light, I squat down, unwrap the test, and dampen the tip. Drivers are blowing their horns, and I'm urinating. I stay squatted down, look at the stripes lining up in the squares, pregnant, not pregnant. Pregnant. Right. I'm going to go home and take a little pill and then call Mother, maybe she can find the words to tell my husband. I'm so sleepy. She's right when she blames me for not sticking to my commitments. I did forget to go to the restaurant for that glass of champagne.

# Letter Time

*A huge* pile of snow has fallen deep inside me. My mother slips this burning pain into my body, I am ready to cry out, the cry will come out later, an infinite cry, it will come out for as long as I live, at a rate of one breath out of every two or three, it will be served to me again and again, this cold abandonment. I can feel it as if someone pressed a wound into my body before the blow fell, the way you trace a pattern in pencil before going over it in ink. It has started, I'm on my way, a ski under each of my soles and ready to take a fall. Standing farther back than the other mothers, she signals goodbye from the sidewalk, she isn't waving her hand, she has turned her head to one side so I won't see her tears, and she is smiling gently, as if there were no point in digging any deeper, as if she knew that a hundred yards from here, in any case, I'll have the wound of her smile in my heart, so it isn't worth raising her arm too high, it's over, the bus is on its way, she disappears. I put my hand on my heart, slip it between the snaps of my parka, and touch my wound. There, just behind my left breast which has not yet begun to grow, a little fissure pulses and I hold the two edges squeezed together, as if, were they to open, I might spill out all over the place, without her.

The day we arrive, at snack time, jam in bowls and aromatic hot milk, the children in a rectangle with a table leader who says, Clear the table! as soon as he's done, or Recess! and then we all spill outside, our mouths still full, our milk hardly swallowed, still in the warm conduit leading to our cold stomachs. But during tea time, before we scatter, the adults come in to hand out the letters. Parents, grandparents, brothers and sisters, even cousins sometimes, send us messages to tell us they love us, are thinking about us, missing us. We just got here, this very morning, our suitcases are still piled in the entrance, but they already miss us. Especially me. I get five letters from my mother. She mailed them before my departure so that I could have them right from the start. That's what they advised during the preliminary meeting. It makes the abandonment feel less extreme. And in my head I'm begging for the distribution to stop. The instructor says my name five times in a row, and all the children burst out laughing. One little girl asks me if all the letters are from my Mommy, but I say no, not only, from a friend, too, a grown-up man who's twenty-something years old, who was hiding behind a tree when we pulled away so as not to scare anyone. Such a difference in age. The little girl shrugs her shoulders, you can probably tell when I'm lying. Letter time becomes the moment of my mortification, everyone mutters my name before the instructor starts handing out the letters. It's impossible to do anything discreetly in this place, everything is everyone's business, there is no way you can hide anything, even our suitcases are searched for candy or cookies so that they'll be shared, we're living in a collective. But luckily my mother hasn't hidden any candy or cookies. Except behind her words; I can find some there, sugar and sweets, words as nourishment, my throat is tight as I read them, she's chosen such cheerful words to tell me she's okay, that everything is fine without me.

One little girl is crying because an instructor has found the zipper hidden in the fur of her stuffed doggie, where her mother had slipped little notes along with pieces of candy, one for each of the twenty nights between now and our return, and the instructor is shouting, This kid hid this from us, and we said we would share the candy! And out loud she reads the mother's notes. The little girl cries for a long time, I go over and sit on her bunk, and for what must be the first time ever I say a bad word out loud, and I say it over and over, I say, That's really shitty, shitty, shitty. The little girl clutches her stuffed doggie to her chest and says it was her hiding place, hers alone and no one else's. I bring her some handkerchiefs so she can stuff her doggie's empty stomach, I'm moved by her tears but I'm pleased that the business with her stuffed doggie made everyone forget the business of my letters for a while. One little boy always mutters the same words before he goes to sleep, the words his mother says to him at night to calm him down, together they learned some sort of poetry where the words would come together in a way to re-create her presence, and in the huge dormitory someone says *shhh* to the boy, and we all laugh and make fun of him and take advantage of the commotion, some to look at a photo of their mother in a little book or a secret diary, some to sniff her perfume on a scrap of handkerchief without anyone seeing. One kid vomits all the way from his top bunk into some brand-new slippers placed by the foot of the bed of the kid who was making fun.

---

In my correspondence I thank my mother politely for her letters, but I try to turn a phrase that will imply not to send them anymore. Up here they cross out in red or white anything that might worry the parents. She doesn't notice, I insist and try everything to make her stop loving me for the duration of these three weeks, I tell her pointless things couched in flat words, and it does seem like I start receiving fewer letters, but right up to the end of our stay the children snigger whenever they hear my name at letter time. For three weeks I've been thinking about running away, or rape, I think I'd rather be raped than to stay here, I figure that after the rape and the hospital she would come. What I wouldn't like is to be raped and then have them bring me back here, without taking me to her, so I escape, I escape with my mind while her ink is flowing, and today I know that I can escape, from anywhere, at any time, I have the excuses, the lies, the means, today I'll run away and no one can hold me prisoner for anything, I am infinitely free, I can leave everything behind, leave everyone at any time, and that is a real prison. Would you believe, I write to my mother now, and she is old and is waiting for my missives from Faucon-de-Barcelonnette. It's a high mountain where I lost my soul and where I decided to try to find it again. Maybe when the snow melts, things might change. For the time being, I still feel abandoned, even on the highest peak.

# There's a Pill for That

I enter the classroom with my butt squeezed tight around my vitamin suppository. I'm sucking on a lozenge of oligo elements with regenerative virtues. If I include drops and my morning tablets, I'm swallowing no less than fourteen doses of medication daily. My mother is doping me, she has ways to make me sleep at night, to wake me in the morning, to make me attentive or drowsy or relaxed, to fill me with composure or arouse my fighting spirit. But there's a problem when I go to spend the weekend at Sophie's: Her mother secretly interrupts my treatment, she thinks that all this medicine is making me stupid. Especially the allergy tablets: She says that trying to fight pollen in December is taking things a bit too far. I feel bad, as if I were betraying my mother by spending a weekend without any medication and then not even getting sick. As for her, I don't know what she's up to when I'm playing outside in the grass, but I'm worried that she's looking at photos of my father or that she's tearing up anything that's left of him. She turns the memories over in her mind, then all of a sudden it gets to her.

Once I'm home, Mom counts and checks, but we were careful to toss out everything she'd given me. So she's pleased, she says she can leave me on my own, that I know how to look after myself, in any case she thinks the Prexiplan may have something to do with it. She asks for news about the Aerist, the Vetalam, and the Maprall syrup, she'd like to know how I'm feeling, she wants to check the effect of all my tablets. They had a good weekend, too. They must be lounging around out in the garden by now, in the rustic sewers of the village of Jaudray. Just like my father, floating along in his little boat, his face lifted to the bright sunshine, no sunscreen, no hat, happily on his own far away from us, savoring the bliss of being newly divorced.

Every illness has its treatment; no sooner have you hinted at some pain or threat than my mother is already elbow deep into her witchcraft. My father left her: She had applied the wrong dosage. Since then she's been more focused, nothing can distract her as she sits bent over her sewing, her newspapers, her medical-product information leaflets. She doesn't work away from home anymore, since he left her, but she never cries. She just goes on hoping that life will prop her up somehow, thanks to her wall of chemistry. I like it when she is doing her research, when she's poisoning me, at least that way she doesn't get sad. It's been going on for two years now, she often compares medicine to a game, sometimes she decides to try a certain treatment because she likes the name of some molecule. A nice little gel capsule alongside an octagonal tablet —and they do exist— can have a very positive side effect.

Nothing positive about me this morning, however, taking my test, sitting on the hot suppository now dribbling inside me. She's found the suppository that makes me lose my concentration but she hasn't found the gel capsule that would help me to assimilate. Even a fraction of Anticossyl seems a nicer prospect than the fraction that is spread across my stenciled test sheet—I'll bet you that it's a diseased fraction, it just has to be, it's enough to drive you crazy it's so hyper-complicated. I'll speak to my mother, she'll take care of my fraction, that will make her feel better. We'll help her get back on her feet, but that poor fraction with a bar right through its stomach, I know what that feels like, how can I make it smile and above all how can I solve it? I write it out, all of a sudden, just as it comes to me, first lines then pages, I hand in a mathematics composition on the disease of the fraction, its distress and discomfort, and I get an F, a warning, and am told to go to the headmaster's office.

The headmaster is acting very headmasterly, I think he must have taken too much of something, he's completely wound up. He says more than once that he thinks I'm totally out to lunch, hammering it into my thick skull, I'll end up with a headache for sure. So I'll take a little pill. Mom doesn't understand why I got an F, so she decides to take me to a psychologist, she says that if I'm getting Fs then we have to fill the gaps in my knowledge so that I can make up all that has been lost without wasting time. She doesn't believe in the virtue of a kick in the ass, which is what the headmaster wanted, and that's fine with me. She says I'm not a robot: That's reassuring. So she makes an appointment right away with that lady who saw me to get me to stop sucking my tongue. It was the dentist who figured that one out. My mother was in a right state. She would explain to guests that when I wasn't sucking I didn't know how to put my tongue back behind the bumps on my palate. And everyone would try to swallow, placing their tongue right where it belonged. And my father would sigh.

My mother is waiting for me in the psychologist's waiting room. The psychologist is a woman with big puffy hair, a necklace, and rings. My mother doesn't wear jewelry now that my father has left. She says it gives her an allergy. When I come back out of the doctor's office my mother decides to apply carefully something she read in a book: She will suggest talking about my session but won't oblige me to. But I do talk about it, since I've got nothing to hide, all I did was tell the psychologist that everything would be fine, because my mother would surely find a remedy for my abysmal incompetence in mathematics, and if need be she'll get some researchers on the case, too.

Since it's raining, Mom gives me an umbrella and a little tablet. She has bought me some water, you can die from asphyxiation if you ingest a tablet without drinking. She makes me gulp down the whole bottle. I'm not thirsty, but you have to keep yourself hydrated between meals, because otherwise during meals you'll start to blow up and your digestion will slow down and anyway that's just how it is. The appointment with the psychologist made us lose an hour in our schedule, so we have to make up for it during bath time,

Mom thinks out loud on the way home, I try to respond, but I realize she's gone inside her own head and she's not coming back out. She's deliberating herself in a way, I know you can't say that, but I don't have a remedy for that particular word.

"Or a shower. A bath will take too long. I should have started running one before going to get her. All we would have had to do was add some hot water."

"No, listen, Mom, I'm not very dirty anyway, I had a sick note so I stayed inside at recess."

"By the sink, then, just quickly, with some towelettes. I'll fix dinner in the meantime, something cold, even though you didn't have any meat at lunch. I'll make a steak tartare."

"I hate red meat."

"And just this once, you won't have to clear the table, you can leave right away and do your teeth, and your poem to learn by heart for tomorrow, and then off to bed."

"Can you cook the steak tartare for me?"

"No. The whole point of a tartare is that you don't waste time. And the blood means vitamins. Okay, that's what we'll do, you take the intimate wipes and run them under your arms, use a face cloth with cold water on your face, which reminds me, I saw a little pimple on you, don't let me forget to take a look at it."

When we get home, she finds the results of my blood test in the mail. Everything is normal. We'll carry on as we began. You see, we're on the right track! she says. She is so pleased that she even grills my ground meat. During dinner Dad calls, she puts him in his place, she says it's absolutely surreal how he always manages to call while we're having dinner, so as a result she doesn't let me speak to him. She gives him a very cool description of my session at the psychologist's, she acts as if she had actually been there. I gulp down my hamburger, but I'm stunned. Eventually she hangs up and says, So there, that should keep him happy.

"I never told the psychologist that I didn't like mathematics because my father is a chemist."

"You didn't? Well, what did you tell her then?"

"I don't have to tell you, remember . . ."

"Oh right, you only tell me about it if you want to. Run off to bed, I'll come tuck you in."

I feel like telling her to shut her big mouth. This is the first time I've ever felt this kind of reaction. I wonder if it isn't the Zorg unhinging me. So I leave the table and go to brush my teeth, like we discussed before we came home. She sends me her praise from the kitchen, reminding me to use the fluoride and take one and a half of the little pills to have sweet pink dreams. We had to increase the dose, I've been taking this one for at least two years and one tablet is no longer enough. I have blue and green dreams, but no more pink dreams at all. And since I have math tomorrow, Mom is giving me a Peps tablet, it's something that's just come out, it's American. She has faith in it, even for the fractions. She shouts to remind me to take that one, too. And I don't know what's come over me, but suddenly I throw the fluoride down the drain, I don't know what's come over me, I do the same thing with the entire contents of the medicine cabinet above the sink, I don't know what's come over me, I call to Mom and show her the bloodbath, I don't know what's come over her, she's calling law enforcement, and she declares that we've been burgled.

Afterward, in tears while we wait for the police, she doesn't even look to see if anything else has been stolen.

"The worst of it is that we have nothing left to get through the night. How are you going to get to sleep? They stole everything."

"Don't worry, Mom."

———

She prowls the corridor first one way then the other, looks on the floor to see if there might be a little scrap of something, a tiny crumb. She runs her finger along the baseboard, the way I used to before she started me on the Valium. Tonight, however, we're just going to have to interrupt the treatment. The police are taking their time. Mom calls again, she's just realized her husband's been stolen as well.

Listen, officer, are you coming or not? All the medication has disappeared and now I see my husband has, too. I don't know in which order, I don't know whether . . .

The police hang up on her. She watches as I suffer and sweat from withdrawal symptoms. She doesn't know where to turn, nor how to calm me down, and I'm sweating, my stomach aches, I feel like crying. I point to the sink, to the empty containers in the wastebasket. She says that only a pervert could do something like this. Not for one second can she accept the idea that I might have done it. She refuses. I show her the wastebasket again, put my hand in it, pull out some blister packs, but instead of understanding, she says again, Yes, I can see, everything is here and everything is empty. She goes back on the warpath down to the end of the hall, she figures there might be a small stock she'd forgotten about tucked away somewhere. I'm trembling all over, I remember now that the product information always says that you have to stop gradually, especially where tranquilizers are concerned. She comes back and hugs me, we sit in the hallway and keep watch for a light, something, a glimmer of hope. She wipes my forehead with a damp cloth, squeezes one of my pimples frenetically, tries to get me to go to bed when she's finished, and for my sweet pink dreams she tells me a story, any old story, but it gets me out of my black hole, I stop trembling and for the first time since my father left, I fall asleep without her slipping substances into my blood to kill me. She stretches out beside me to listen to my breathing. She is crying, she says that now she knows, now she realizes that Dad has left.

Tomorrow she'll go to work. While she was falling asleep, she promised.

The next morning she gets mad and suspects that I'm the one who threw out all the tablets. She's puzzled, wonders what came over me, but calms down quickly enough and runs out to buy some enemas. She thinks that the Propenton must have reacted with the Alatrask. To counterbalance, all that's needed is a good purge.

# You'll Be a Woman, My Girl

*The* parties have changed, dollies' tea sets replaced by rock music. The mother is trying to put lipstick on her daughter, but the girl resists, pinches her lips, says she wants to choose her clothes for the party herself and her mother knows the girl will end up, as always, in her sweatsuit. It's enough to make her disgusted that she ever had a daughter. With her grown-up sons she had to put up with skateboards and potato chips and hair gel on her comb and sticky fingerprints on her sofas, but she'll be damned if her youngest child will behave like that. She's going to take things in hand. No way will she allow the child to keep coming home from parties with a grin on her face because she lifted and carried the boys during the slow dances since she's bigger than average for her age. Just imagining her daughter picking up some little guy to swing him round is enough to make her dizzy. She's already used the pretext of her daughter's poor grades in math to stop her from playing basketball. Instead, she's taking private lessons with a pretty young student, who may not be up to scratch as far as teaching is concerned but she knows how to dress and make herself attractive. The mother is counting on her to tell her daughter about all her little love affairs, after all they're not that far apart in age, and the student isn't the type to lift a boy when she's dancing. To keep a man—and the mother knows what she's talking about—the best thing is to work on one's body relentlessly, and once it's perfect, to offer it, delicately.

To no avail. The girl continues to swear by her baggy boxer shorts and bras that squash her budding breasts. The mother takes her husband aside, explains her despair to him yet again, and he says it will come eventually: Femininity is not automatic.

"Help me to nudge her into it," says the mother.

"Oh, come on, let her be a teenager, try to find herself."

"Can't you see she looks like a boy? And now she wants her hair cut short—even asked me to pay for it."

"Well, it is the fashion, just let her, it will grow out."

"And I don't know if you've noticed, but her breasts are tiny."

"Maybe they haven't finished growing, and they're very pretty as they are."

"Yeah, yeah, yeah."

The mother gives her daughter sidelong looks and often punishes her for swear words that in fact aren't swear words, just expressions she's picked up from her brothers, so the girl begins to languish, feeling bruised, insulted. In spite of everything, she wants her mother to like her. She brings home good grades, her mother looks away; she talks to her about her day, her mother bangs her wooden spoon against the side of a saucepan. The daughter buys flowers, the mother sighs as she accepts them, then tosses them out before they have a chance to wilt. The daughter eventually forgets what her mother's smile was like, yet glimpses it from time to time conferred upon the little twelve-year-old neighbor who has just recorded her own CD and braids her hair into two plaits on either side of her face. So for her birthday the lost daughter asks to have a breast enhancement operation and, wonder of wonders, it works. Her mother smiles and, best of all, agrees to it.

The daughter is seventeen and has gigantic breasts. The mother encourages her daughter to continue with her transformation and offers her collections of lingerie. She buys the panties too big so that the girl herself will realize that there's something weird going on between the top and the bottom. The daughter asks to have her butt surgically sculpted. And the mother offers her some gym and modeling sessions. The daughter shortens her long skirts; the mother is jubilant.

The daughter fails her final year, and the mother is pleased. A woman will find a husband, no need to repeat the year, the main thing is to know how to speak a few languages so they can travel. She sends her to Italy, to be a waitress in a bar. A daytime bar, of course, the daughter can do what she likes at night. All alone, she meets Rico, an Italian Frenchman, who wastes no time offering her a job working with him in the entertainment business, and in France. She comes back from Italy, introduces him to her mother, who finds him to her liking.

"What sort of entertainment are you in?" asks the father.

"Female wrestling."

"But that's a man's sport!" cries the mother.

"No, it's a woman's sport, a particular kind of wrestling, it drives the men wild, it's like a form of dance, at nightclubs."

"Oh, well, if there's dancing involved, that's all right then," says the mother, reassured, then she turns to her husband and says, "What do you think, dear?"

And the husband nods, he is so relieved that his wife—now that their daughter is a real girl at last—is once again a woman in love. And anyway, this wrestling dance must really be something else.

The daughter leaves by car, sitting next to Rico, and the mother is in raptures over his coupé. She's already looking forward to the idea of a wedding. But, thinks the mother as she drops off to sleep, to get to that point she will have to know how to come on strong to him, I don't like the way she walks, like some cowboy, I'll have to let her know, I'll have to show her how to sway her hips. Men can't stand walking around with women who don't know how to sashay. Sunday's a good day to show her how to run her tongue over her lips and her hand through her hair, and then how to sit and spread her legs ever so slightly, hardly at all, I don't mean she ought to become debauched, just know how to do it for the man who's with her without anyone else noticing. Yes, when she comes back on Sunday I'll show her how to use her hands and how to place them on the man so he won't get away. I'll get it, my princess wedding and my dress, thinks the mother as she nods off.

Six months now, every evening ends up with caring for her skin, irritated by the hot cabbage. Wrestling in sauerkraut every night makes the daughter cry, and the burning sensation and exhaustion can only be relieved with a sausage, so as part of the act the daughter rubs herself with a long, spicy Montbéliard sausage, and for a brief while it calms the acidity of the cabbage, so what if the crowd gets excited, goes wild, into a frenzy of delight, and the mother is pleased, she comes from time to time to watch the show and she always manages to let drop that she's the girl's mother. Rico has hired three other girls; the four of them charge at one another in the sauerkraut and they're a huge success, well just look how he's bought himself a second coupé, a coat, and a pied-à-terre with trees all around. After the show the wrestlers apologize for hitting each other and rub cream all over each other's bodies. Tonight, feeling tired as she leaves the disco in Pont d'Orly, the daughter sees Rico kissing another woman. So she heads in the direction of Orly, maybe there's a plane she can take, she'd like to find a new destination, she's tired of Frankfurt and Strasbourg. She's walking along the shoulder of the road, but some spectators who'd enjoyed the show catch up with her, yelling or trying to talk to her about sausages, she can't hear very well, not everything, because of the cabbage, it even gets into your ears and sticks to your hair, just like the warm liquid the men squirt all over her, calling her Hot Blood Pudding, before they finish her off with the help of an iron bar.

On Sunday when the mother came to the morgue to identify her daughter, she was outraged. All she said was that it was not her daughter, her daughter was a real woman, an attractive woman, whom she had helped to create, a woman who would never have tolerated going to her grave with greasy hair.

# Liar

*I feel* hurt, that's all. I'm not going to make a big deal out of it, I'm not going to change her, I'll even keep her until my emancipation, but I do find it would have been more honest on her part simply to tell me the truth. She manipulated me. Ordinarily, you confess to something like that when the child is still quite small—well, actually, it isn't even a confession, it's a statement, I was adopted. It seems it's about time she told me. She's the one who's making a big deal out of it, it's not my fault if things feel weird. I'm ready to put up with whatever comes my way. It makes no difference to me, this mother or another one, so long as I am loved, fed, and housed. I'm just saying that I would have liked to have heard her story. Did she choose me among the other babies in a country orphanage, did someone in charge pull strings so she could get a girl rather than a boy, might she even have paid with her body to get me when I was just a few months old? I couldn't have been very old at all, since I don't remember a thing.

The other day she showed me one of my very first pairs of pajamas, so she said, I checked, size six months. She was so moved it was almost grotesque, but now I can better understand why. The pajamas must have reminded her of the line of people waiting outside the nursery where she saw me, or picked me, there we are on that topic again, what do I know; she must have been there, trembling, with that smile of hers when everything is going wrong, twisting the terry-cloth of the little undershirt she'd planned to put on me as soon as I was hers. She also pulled out a bonnet and some little baby booties that her mother had knit, so the lie is in the whole family. And it's not something they're just hiding, it's completely staged. Was Granny there, too, waiting in the car to adjust the heating so that I'd make my entrance into family life at the right temperature? And where was Daddy? Was he smoking on the sidewalk or fiddling with the other foot of the flowered sleep suit, at the risk of being denied custody of the child for anxious behavior? Did Mom point that out to him and tell him to behave himself? And me, in my cradle, was I sleeping or was I awake, did I scream when I saw this stranger who all of a sudden lifted me up in her arms?

This is getting on my nerves. I'm too old to be throwing tantrums but I am finding it hard to keep quiet about this. When my mother says that I really take after my father the way I sniff the food in my plate, I feel like spilling it all into her lap. I wish she would at least have the decency not to make fun of me openly, she's caused enough harm as it is. I'm at least tactful enough to keep what I know to myself, but it's still not my role to be the one maintaining this fragile balance between us; if she starts trying to get my goat with her little remarks, I'm going to blow it all wide open and tell her that I know. Look at her so proud when she dresses me up like a doll and shows me off, well she'd better not be surprised if one day, in front of a shopkeeper, I start acting all formal with her and calling her Madam. It is all becoming crystal clear. The other evening she was speaking some foreign language with a friend, and pointed to her stomach.

"Why aren't you speaking French?" I asked.

"Darling, Edith just asked me how to say 'savory tart' in English."

"Well it took awfully long just to say 'savory tart' in English."

Believe it or not, the two shrews laughed, and my mother sent me sweetly packing to my bedroom, thrusting the plate of cookies that was next to the teapot into my hands. Guilt, obviously. A classic reaction. In her shoes, I would feel really guilty, too, if I were gossiping with a friend about my adoptive daughter and, on top of it, calling her a savory tart. If I'm not careful, her guilt will make me obese. Which reminds me, here, Lulu, have a cookie if you like. How old are you, anyway? If I don't multiply by seven, you're six years old. Six years less than me, right? And two paws more. So, you weren't here yet when they had me. You are lucky, I can tell you where you're from. You were in a cage at the market, and Mom thought you were really nice, so Daddy bought you. I don't know how much you cost, could be you cost a lot more than I did, the vendor was selling you as pedigreed; which reminds me, I don't want to hurt your feelings, but Mom can't stop making fun of the way your tail curls up at the end, so yes, my dear, you must be a mongrel. Welcome to the club.

———

72

She won't confess, she lies through her teeth all the time. Like when I leave school on Friday with the Mother's Day present that won't fit in my schoolbag and that she can see perfectly well, she acts all surprised when I give it to her on Sunday. Another time I was setting the table, to make a good impression, and all of a sudden I got really worried that before summer she would put me back wherever it was she had found me. She walked past me down the hall and looked at me, I could see that she was looking at me, and then she came back ten minutes later acting as if this were something absolutely astonishing. What a lovely surprise, sweetheart! she exclaimed.

If I were my father, well, if I were her husband, I'd be worried with a liar like that for a wife. She lies to him, too, and asks for my help on top of it. Don't tell Daddy, she murmured, when I was late for school, he'll box my ears. Don't tell Daddy I made that chestnut cake he likes so much, I'll hide it on the top shelf in the cupboard, okay? Don't go and tell Daddy that his brother called about Saturday, he'd figure out there's a surprise in store. Don't tell Daddy we went to the gun shop, he'd guess it's for his birthday.

Why a gun?

My mother wants to kill me. She can't go on living a lie.

I will go to my death with my secret. You'll keep it, won't you, Lulu? But, someday, you'll tell the whole world how suddenly I found the final proof that I'd been adopted: I have brown hair and my mother is blond.

"Yes! I'm coming!"

My mother has something to tell me, you coming, Lulu?

A little sister, won't that be awful? Are we going to get her at the same place you got me? Can I see? No? Why not? Why should I have to wait here? In five months? But why the hospital? Are you getting a sick one? Aren't there any others?

Okay. Right. I'll wait here. I'll make a savory tart.

Now? You're going to the hairdresser's now? What about your color? Roots? What do you mean by roots? Show me!

Well, I never. Lulu, believe it or not, but it's as if under your yellow fur you had black fur. My mother paints her hair yellow. She really is a first-class liar. A liar to the very roots of her hair.

And where are my roots?

# A Pink Baby

*When* I arrived at the clinic I saw a young mother who'd just given birth, wearing a shapeless nightshirt with a giraffe on it. Later, when the child looks at photos of his birth, it's the giraffe he'll go crazy about, not his mother. So I decided to wear something special for the photographer, too. My nightgown is sea green, with *broderie anglaise* on the straps and a drawstring just below my breasts so as not to press on the hollow stomach that has just replaced my hard stomach. I'm in the bed, my knee peeking out of the sheets, and the baby is at my left breast on her back, stretching like a cat. Even the photographer said it was the prettiest shot of the day. And he says I'm a regular sunbeam.

When he's gone, a friend calls me to ask how many stitches I had, six or seven, I'm not sure exactly. She advises me not to refrain from going to the toilet, something that wouldn't have occurred to me. After I've hung up I realize that she didn't even ask the baby's name.

I'm looking. For a name, that is. I like Lili, but I don't know if I can use it on its own or if it's just a nickname, and I don't like the idea of calling my daughter Liliane one bit. Then there's Marguerite and Pamela, but I'll get tired of those names, I can tell. And I don't like those double names that you could go back and forth between. I have a soft spot for Jacques, but for a girl it's not very common. If her father were here, maybe the two of us together could come up with something, but he doesn't know I've just given birth. He often travels for long periods. The last time he left, I was four months pregnant. I was wearing belts and tried to make him believe, jokingly, that I was having trouble with wind because of all the planes he was taking. I didn't say a thing about being pregnant, I was afraid that if he found out he wouldn't come back. Since his name is Jules, I could call our daughter Juliette. Who knows, it might even mollify him. He doesn't like children, but I don't think that's really the problem. He doesn't like the idea of having a child because he doesn't like his last name and because he's the only male descendant, he's decided not to pass it on so that it will disappear. It's lucky I've had a daughter. So his name won't have to be used for too long, twenty, twenty-five years at the most, and then she'll find someone to put a ring on her finger. And that will be that.

While I was expecting the baby, one of my friends was obsessed with knowing whether it would be pink or blue, but the problem with my secret is that Jules only ever looks at black or yellow children, he finds them much more interesting than white kids. One day he told me how he was walking around and he went up to a little black kid with a big schoolbag and said, "Boo." The kid turned around, gave him a dark look, and went on his way with a shrug of his shoulders. Jules is sure that a little white kid would have started crying and his mother would have started shouting. While he's climbing around mountains in search of mystery, that's the picture of mothers he carries around with him. He's due back soon, he said four months and it's already been almost five; I'll have to tell him about little Molly's birth. No, Molly's no good, there's no reason for me to call her Molly. I think I'll go buy a big dog and get my ear tattooed, and then maybe my baby won't be as noticeable.

Maybe an African or Asian name like Matou or Comnet

could make him forget she's white? Out of respect for her
father's taste, I made sure her first pajamas would have black
and yellow stripes, I found some in a costume store, I just cut
off the little bee's wings. Maya is sleeping in her cradle, she
has long fingernails, they told me they'd fall off and I don't
need to cut them. A friend suggested I chew them, to create
yet another bond between us, one that would come quicker
and stronger, but I don't like to think about that part of it, it
moves me a little too much, it might upset me entirely. Already, when the nurse asked me, So, are we breast-feeding?
I asked who and what. And anyway, what business is it of
hers? She wanted to know if she had to give me tablets to
prevent the milk from rising or if we would just let it happen. So, we just let it happen, I didn't dare say no, I saw that
it was something you're not supposed to mess with. Along
came the milk, and now my breasts are even heavier and
harder, and I have rings on my shirts. I cut a washcloth in
two and I cover each breast with them as soon as Anna has
finished feeding. The terrycloth gets damp, I go and rinse
out the cloth and a grayish liquid dribbles down the drain.
When my daughter Emeline takes my breast I find it so
touching, said the friend who didn't even ask me the baby's
name, so I explained to her that I was indeed very moved,
but there's something wrong about it, it paralyzes me. I don't

know if I'm supposed to squeeze my breast or not, like the washcloth or a cow's udder, and I don't dare ask, so I just don't move, I just hold Marie's head on my chest, it's glued there the way I glue Jules's head to my lips, and I wait and think about something neutral, a landscape or a string of words. And then it's burp time. The first time, the nurse applauded, I hid behind my hair, and she asked me if I'd heard it. Well, yes, it's not exactly easy to ignore a barfly after he's had two or three beers. When I put Corine back into her crib, my stomach was all wet. She got me all hot, Edwige, sucking on my breast like that. Inès went to sleep but I was the one who was tired.

During labor, I called Jules, but his phone wasn't working. No voice mail in the depths of his Amazonian jungle. I figured that if I was talking to him I wouldn't be shouting at the nurses, it really bothered me to be calling the midwife a bitch. And in between insults I said sorry, and a nurse's aide said it wasn't a problem, they were used to it. So at one point I called her a slut. I'd managed to hold it in until then, but since she said to go right ahead: Get your hand away from there, you filthy slut! She was pressing on my stomach to get Emilie to move down, and inside it felt like someone was stabbing my flesh with a carving fork.

———

Sophie is fast asleep. I'm incredibly sad, all alone in the white bed, with the sound of the carts in the corridor, and women screaming, and children falling. At noon they gave me a soup with stringy little noodles in it. I thought about Christine, who someday will surely have germs in her body. I thought about Elizabeth's first day of school, weeping on the sidewalk, crying that she doesn't want to go, I thought about Esther's first lies, her hidden report card, her lost gym bag, her bad grade in conduct, for cheating. I thought about Brigitte, out in the yard, Brigitte and the pebbles she talks to, there's the daddy and the mommy and the children, off we go, let's play, all alone without any friends. I thought about Sylvie and how her curvature of the spine makes her suffer, how I have to write excuses and keep her covered and give her massages, she can't manage on her own, I help her, put a Band-Aid on the finger she chews on, a bandage on the foot she's just twisted, a neck brace on her latest injury. I think about Eglantine, always first in everything, even gym, she doesn't like cuddles, she'll get married at sixteen and Jules will be happy. I think about Antigone, who wants to go into theater, everybody thinks that's normal except Jules, who thinks before you get so excited about something you should study for your finals, and I agree, I'm even nodding my head, and Antigone, furious, leaves the living room and says, You make me sick. I think about Ingrid, misunderstood, bulimic, who vomits into the toilet bowl everything I work myself into the ground to prepare, all she likes now is hot water, it makes it easier to puke, she says. I think about Doris, who searches for the meaning of things, of people, who invents operating instructions, reads essays, takes notes, follows examples, runs away, ends up writing books and committing suicide. I think about Chloé, carried off by cancer; and Marianne, who runs away and is discovered drowned; and Valérie, who tells me I'm not her mother anymore; and Karine, who can't leave because she's afraid to leave me, she doesn't want me to be unhappy; I think about Cécile, who ends up an old maid because of me. I think about Prune, who makes up illnesses, and Annie, who'll bring some home to us if she keeps sleeping around like that. I think about Laetitia, who smells of cigarettes, and the crook of her arms is blue, and one day there's a shiner around her lovely eyes, and she swears it was the door.

I look at the door to this room, opening from time to time to let in a small person who asks how things are and inspects the baby. I try out names, but people frown. It always reminds them of someone, and it's no good. My phone lights up with a message from Jules. He says, I'll be there tomorrow,

and then, I'm thinking about you. I look below the drawstring on my nightgown, I prod my soft stomach, try to suck
it in, I want to be able to hide it for tomorrow. Vanessa is still
sleeping, with her little fists held tight on either side of her
head, I think about Jules when he says that life is beautiful
and he makes a gesture a bit like that one, which means
hurrah, or at least I think it does. Tomorrow I'll buy him a
steak, when he comes back from his trips he asks for meat,
and then for his little woman. I'll make French fries—so
what about the smell—and strawberry soup, if I can find any
strawberries in February. Which makes me think, Bénédicte
is a Pisces. I don't know her rising sign, but someday she's
bound to ask me the hour of her birth so she can find it for
herself. And she'll say, Oh, how awful, I've got Scorpio rising, just like you! I'll send her to her room to copy out a
thousand times, LITTLE GIRLS MUST LOVE THEIR MOTHERS.
Titine is annoying me now, lying there in her plastic box
with her last name on it, but no first name in front since
I haven't found one. She weighs six and a half pounds,
Loulotte. A fine baby.

But I'd better get going, I've got the housework to finish, the
puddle of water to remove from the carpet in the foyer. I
want to go home, I'm expecting my Jules, the way you ex-

pect a child, with my hand on my tummy, wanting to tell him I'm here, soothe him, everything will be nice and quiet. Nénette is fast asleep. I get up and collect my things. I'm going to leave the hospital, they'll know where to place her, and things will be a lot less complicated without a first name. I'll go to a liposuction clinic, Jules is coming home tomorrow, he'll find me changed, but I'll tell him that he was gone a long time, and that really shook me up. If he notices my stitches, I'll tell him I had a fall. Bye. Bye. Baby.

# The Breakup

$\mathcal{My}$ mother gets on my nerves. She knows I think she's boring, so that makes her aggressive. I've decided to stop seeing her. It's like my bank account, there's nothing going on with her, it's all just stagnating. She's getting old, I'm getting mature. And yet I do make an effort, I try to get her to think about something else besides her games. Always the same thing, her TV games or the ones in the magazines, on cheese boxes, on packets of Kleenex, in supermarkets. Aside from that, nothing interests her, except the unexpected deaths of famous people. I'm studying to become a statutory auditor, and she thinks that's something to do with art. The other day I heard her on the phone saying that it didn't sound like a profession for a woman and that I'd probably ruin my health, all that working with chisels and stone and dust, given my fragile build. She had a worried look on her face so I tried to tell her more about my profession. She listened, but as usual she ended our exchange saying something that had nothing to do with the topic at hand. Some story about a new nail clipper to cut the cat's claws. I pointed out that she was forever interrupting me with stupid stuff, that I could never have a real conversation with her, so then she said that we couldn't spend all day nitpicking and quibbling. She was hurt and made fun of me, calling me Miss Accounting Department and offering to go to the basement to look for my old abacus. That's how it goes whenever I try to get her to talk about something else besides her earning loyalty points, well, *earning* might be saying a bit much, given the fortune she wastes on stamps hoping to win some prize that is always missing either batteries or parts. I don't know why I go to such lengths to talk to her, my life doesn't interest her. She's only interested in making sure that boys bring me home when they take me out. If I talk about one of them in greater detail, she says that she is worried about my vaccinations. If I organize a trip abroad with a girlfriend, especially if it's a girlfriend I've already mentioned a few times, she says, Who is that girl, already? or Who is that girl, again? Then she goes on about repatriation insurance, in case of illness or death. Or about some other country much better than the one where I'm going, somewhere much more interesting and much more pleasant. I think I'm going to stop calling her.

When I was little, we got along well. In the evening we'd look through guidebooks and tell my father that we'd like to go here or there, and so he'd take us. We didn't have to insist for very long. But later my mother seemed to shrink suddenly, to change countries. Her country is impenetrable, she's crouching in the shadow of some boundless misery. I'm going to stop seeing her.

A few months ago I went to live on my own, and at the time my decision didn't seem to bother her, but all of a sudden she shifted into a strange state, as if my absence were equivalent to a disappearance and I had to be removed from the landscape at all costs, as if it would be better for everyone if I had never existed. And yet I still do go to see her often, so that she won't miss me too much, even if I do get bored. I think she's bored, too, because she hardly lifts her nose from her newspapers, or only does so she can tell me I'm not looking my usual self and that I must not be eating properly. I will admit that she does light up if I suggest we go out somewhere, and she rushes off to put her makeup on as if she were going to a dinner party, then in the street she suddenly speeds up, darting off this way or that. She's all over the place, even her words trip over one another. It's as if so much time spent playing games has made her lose all sense of reality, as if she's come up with an imaginary language, impenetrable to anyone who doesn't share our blood:

"And what about, in the gallery, the flies, you know, there, with the barrette?"

"Maybe, yes."

"No, we'll find it first, try it, the round tablecloth, but as for the socks, I think the size is too big, those blinds, make them in paper, well, for the bedroom, to match the towels."

So I get even more worried. Going out just arouses too many emotions and she can't get her words out fast enough. During the sales it's a disaster. All her words already higgledy-piggledy and now she adds figures, discounts and percentages, all that's left for me to do is plug my ears and wait. Sometimes I tell Dad about it, but he says everything is fine, she's happy, that's all, he says that I'm the one who's splitting hairs. I can't understand a thing she's saying anymore, but yes, everything is fine. I'm going to stop taking her out now, too, that's final. Listening to her is bad for me, but taking her out is destroying me. I call her back, I've got to try and understand why I feel this way and explain to her exactly why I am going to stop calling her, soon.

"You know, the wallpaper, the lady came by and her husband has the time, but not before January because of the transition. It's pretty brave, Tanzania, when you think of it."

"I don't understand a thing you're saying, Mom."

"Well, of course not, you're not listening."

So I try to do a better job of listening and think about it like a puzzle, but I think she is deliberately swallowing bits here and there. It's up to me to find them, to make them up, to make up my mother, to find the time it takes to make a success of her. I suspect she may be frittering herself away just to keep me busy. While I'm studying for my exams, she calls me:

"Sorry to bother you, but I'll be quick. Are you coming this weekend? Because there are our cousins in Colmar, but we'll only go there if you're not coming, if you come, we'll stay, just say whether you'd like quiche or meat. Never mind about the baptism."

"No, that's fine, go ahead to the baptism. That way you'll see the sea."

"We'll see what we want to see."

She doesn't even correct me about Colmar being near the sea. But she does talk back. This is persecution. I will never speak to my mother again. But just before I stop forever, I call her, one last time. I know she's going to reply by going off on a tangent, but I'd like to know what she thinks of the way my new fiancé reacted. I'm giving her a chance to raise her eyes from her missing words.

"He told me he'd prefer to go sailing on his own this summer, rather than take me with him."

"He's cheating on you."

"Do you think so? But if he were, he'd just drop me, he wouldn't go to all this bother to lie, don't you think?"

"You think he's going to a lot of bother? You're not hard to please."

"No, but he could easily just simply say it's all over."

"It's not all over, he wants to keep both of you in a loving mood."

"What's that supposed to mean?"

"He's keeping you on the back burner. At the same time, he's having fun. It's what you do at that age, you know!"

"Should I leave him, you think? Maybe that will give him a sort of wake-up call?"

"For that to happen, he'd need to have a brain."

Whenever there's an emergency, my mother knows just what to say to bring you right down, it's impossible to be around her, I've got to break it off, she's sadistic. Even her suffering is calculated. I can see where my love of figures comes from. If I tell her as much, if I even try to suggest that something intriguing is going on, like this coincidence with my love of figures and her pleasure in calculating, she'll just say, Huh? or, Entrepreneurial mortician in ten letters, must be undertaker, no?

This evening I don't call her, I go straight to bed and once I'm there I think about my boyfriend who's going to go sailing on his own because he likes to, and that's that. What a loser. I don't know why my mother has to take me for an imbecile. I'm leaving him. Obviously. I don't need her to help me come to that conclusion. I have a brain.

I can't sleep with these useless curtains, they don't do a thing to hide the light from the street and the cars, I'll have to line them. She's been telling me to do it for ages, but I don't know how. And I won't ask her. I'm glad I haven't called her all day, I'm forgetting her. In another few weeks it will be as if I'd never had a mother. She's surely in bed by now and telling Dad that I didn't call. If she thinks I'm throwing a little tantrum over nothing, she's in for a major surprise tomorrow. I won't tell her that earlier today a boy quoted Dick Rivers to me. At the university cafeteria, he said, Everything inside your jeans will be inside my bed tonight. Well, my mother won't know a thing about it. I'm going to keep my poet to myself. What does she think? That I'm so clueless I don't know that going off sailing on his own means he's leaving me? I wasn't born yesterday. Tonight I won't call, but tomorrow I will, at least to tell her that. As for this new boy, I hope he'll quote that song to me again. I don't know what Mom would say about a boy who's blunt and witty, but I'm not interested anyway. She'd advise me to make myself desirable, what the hell does she know about that, inaccessible fortress that she is? She'll only start talking to me about her ancestors or her classmates, but what do I care about those people? I don't know them. And if I did I'd have no trouble telling them exactly where to get off.

This morning I called her to break it off, she picked up:

"Make it quick, you're bothering me, I've got to put the groceries away."

"I just wanted to send you a kiss."

# With Affectionate Kisses

*In* front of or behind the window, depending on the season, they put me in this chair from dawn to dusk, and sooner or later, depending on the season, I start throwing stones. They never reach the wall surrounding the little garden where the grass grows—wild in summer, mown low in winter, as if doing penance. I mustn't move, I am waiting for a girl, soon it will be time, and everything will be fine. She is going to come, go, come, with her lovely hands, her eyes, and her white skin, what will they be like this time. A girl will walk in the garden, will look at the grass or the earth, will be interested in stars and stories. I'll tell her about the meteors, the way my father used to, the way her father used to, I've never known how to explain to men that they should be quiet and, above all, not speak after my father has spoken. My granddaughter is coming and I will recite the Lord's Prayer to her.

It's almost three o'clock and they sit us in a circle, all together, all these expectant mothers, suspended between the tick of the clock and the moment when water—like our feelings—will inevitably spill out under us. They'll mop it up. While we wait for our visits we sing, and when the doors open and the children come, for some of us there will be so much joy, for others, so much of a wait, and one fear—to have been forgotten. But maybe they'll come next week, say the caregivers. You can't even tell who's crying, the children or the mothers, some are laughing, others complaining. It's hard to have a daughter. I'm waiting for her, she's different, indifferent, hopefully she's regained her self-composure and her grace.

There are always at least nine months between any two visits from my daughter. It's her husband who's reluctant, I think he doesn't like the hospice. As for coming on her own, without him—she gave it a lot of thought, but 125 miles without a copilot is particularly dangerous when you're on tranquilizers, even occasionally. So she calls me, hesitates, promises to come and then is delayed, and when at last she comes she says, You see, I'm here. For them it's a day out. She calls the night before to tell me she'll be there the next day. He's agreed but if it's sunny he'll reproach her for not waiting for a rainy Sunday, and she replies that she's not a meteorologist. His name is Jean but she calls him Jean-Lou. I can't understand why she never abbreviates a thing, never, not even with me, she calls me Mommy Lucie, as if she had other mothers somewhere else. Her children don't write often but they write well, you can tell that she's had something to do with the style and the feeling in their letters. I can sense her there, hiding behind the adjective that describes their closing kisses.

When she comes into the garden she waves to me, as if I were a little girl on the far side of the school yard, as if I were about to get up out of my chair and run over to her. So I watch her coming, her face streaked with an ugly scar, because Jean-Lou has taken away her smile. He persuaded her to have her skin stretched so she would look a bit younger. No matter how she tries to make me believe in how filled with fun and enjoyment their everyday life is, no matter how enthusiastically she describes a play they've seen or a ring he's given her or a dream they've had, I can see her fading, like a plant that has been overnourished, is spoiled, is withering. He walks behind her, with the boy and girl, as if rehearsing for the joyful and wonderful destiny that is approaching, the day I die. I doubt it will be wonderful, but at least the hospice isn't costly. I'm the one who refused to go to the classy place higher up in the village, it would have cost a great deal more, and I preferred to bank on the visit of my loved ones in a humble retreat that wouldn't take anything away from them. Well, yes, it will if I hang on too long, but that's not my intention. Yesterday they found a little lump in my back. With the one in my breast and the little one below my ear that I had already discovered before they biopsied it, I don't give myself too much longer. I would like, just once, before I go, for my daughter to come all by herself and smile at me, the way she used to, with her lip raised above her front teeth, and not as if she had just swallowed a knife. It's not her fault, she loved her father, she tried in vain to find someone just like him and, disappointed that there was no one anywhere on earth, she chose Jean-Lou. Afterward she tried to become an ideal wife, using me as her example, but it had been an easy job for me with her wonderful father. It's not her fault, and she's walking up to me, her head bent slightly and her mouth half open. She says hello again, and the children do, too, and I hear my little neighbor Camille, Camille Lartigue, going pee right next to us, right on her seat, the way she always does, she doesn't like visits, she never gets any, so I share mine, thanks to my daughter, who's sophisticated and never forgets to talk to her, And you, Madame Lartigue, have you been enjoying the sunshine this morning? You have to get out, it's good for your morale! and look at all these little sunbeams who are here to see you . . . My grandchildren reluctantly shake hands with my old neighbor. That's when I put myself in Camille's shoes, she's pissing and at the same time listening to a woman thirty years younger than her who looks every bit as old, and who's telling her that the sun has come to visit her. The children burst out laughing, move a few feet away and hold their nose. My daughter cannot stand this pee business, moreover she always checks to be sure I've been given my quota of diapers, she's the one who pays for them, after all. Well, with Jean-Lou, and they don't like it one bit if I'm being given three diapers when they've been paying for four, and that's perfectly normal. If need be, they'll go to five, all I have to do is ask. After the diaper business, discussed in hushed voices, it seems hard to speak. The children are turning round in circles, aimlessly, squabbling amid the wheelchairs, canes, and glasses of water. No shortage, then, of threats

and smacks. Jean-Lou demonstrates his authority, with a
weary smile my daughter confirms that she is on his side,
then looks at me to see if I am following the conversation.
Then they are pleased, I smile first to one, then another, say
thank you for the slice of pear clafoutis in a plastic box that
she is going to take home after I've eaten some. Yuck, the
children will say. My daughter gets on her high horse, she'd
rather I say thank you to the children than to the slice of
cake. They're the ones who made it. I'm rattling on deliberately, and it reassures her, confirms her belief that she was
right to put me here, it's liberating, a relief to her. When her
husband says that I'm nicely settled, she'll be able to reply
honestly that they have done a good job. Especially Madame
Lartigue, the kids will add, snickering, she did a real good
job!

I'm watching for my daughter's smile, the one she had as a
child when she posed so sweetly for photographs, in my
arms. I'm looking deep in her eyes for the ghost of a mem-
ory, but she's forgotten, her face is in shock, frozen by a
larger drama. She knows I'm looking at her, so she is trying
to make sure I'm not seized up or something like that due to
my old age, something that would take up her time. She
touches my arm, asks if I'm all right. I don't dare ask her to

smile the way she used to, I know she'll just say something like, Oh, for goodness' sake, Mommy Lucie! The children are getting impatient, we're talking vaguely about cousins, about what I eat here, and the children say that I'm really lucky to have so much pasta. If they're very good, all their lives, they'll end up here, if they work hard at loving and doing good, at smiling and making others smile, someday they, too, will eat a lot of pasta. My daughter knows what I am thinking, perhaps even what I keep from saying, so she looks away and smiles at Jean-Lou to show me that it's fine, everything is fine, I can go now.

My little girl is moving down the aisle in the church, behind my large coffin; she chose oak. The children aren't here, they're at summer camp, and Jean-Lou is on call, the very idea, going and dying like that in the middle of the summer, he'll be with us in his thoughts. My daughter drove all the way on her own. She sits down by the coffin where I am at rest. She is astonished to see how small I've become, how shrunken, lying here. She has chosen a prayer that she used to like to sing with her father, so she slips down on her knees, right up close, and puts her hand against the wood. Behind us the other mourners sing along, people from the hospice have written a few words, they've fashioned letters from flowers. The priest sends me off to heaven, then comes over to my daughter. He touches her cheek and caresses her gently, then places his hand with hers on the wood, so she smiles, like an infant who has just taken its first step, like a woman who had lost her grip and then just found it again. She has a broad, dreamy smile on her face, like she used to when she was a child and would look at her father and me, holding each of us by the hand on either side, and she would check to see whether we weighed the same in her little hands, even if Daddy was always a little bit heavier. She smiles and her smile relaxes the muscles in her face, although there's always a chance that fear might suddenly take hold of her features, but she thinks that does not really matter, she is hurting and it is beautiful, she is the only one who falls to her knees, bending over my tomb, she is smiling so hard, says Mommy so quietly, she says no, no, Mommy, and for me that's as good as every unflinching yes she gives to those who don't deserve her. Crouched down on the ground she cries and softly promises, smiling, to come back often. She was in charge, alone at the controls, and she could feel herself take flight. So I leave in peace. A first step: That is what this feels like, and I have the feeling we've passed through it together.

# Munchhausen Syndrome by Proxy

*The* moment we arrive at the hospital, she painstakingly cleans the furniture with alcohol and pays for television access, wrapping the remote control in a shower cap. She hugs Mrs. Domini, the head nurse who is in charge of the floor and knows us well, my mother and me, since we've been coming here for a year. I'm very weak when we arrive, my legs are wobbly, my mouth is dry, and my mother often has to carry me up the stairs, then she lays me out on a stretcher. At last she can catch her breath, they'll take care of me and reassure her. My illness is driving the doctors crazy, they cannot understand why I keep getting septicemia, it's not as if I had any autoimmune deficiency, and my food is always carefully chosen by Mother herself, she watches over me.

She amazes the doctors with how much she knows, they even call her Doctor, she blushes and denies it. She was an assistant pharmacist but, ever since I started getting sick, she stopped work to devote herself to me, in spite of all the sighing and tutting of her girlfriends, who were against the idea.

She goes with me into the radiology room, stands behind the glass, doesn't miss a word of what the doctors are saying while they're taking the X-rays, then she comes to the door of the examining room, they give her white scrubs and a mask so she can hold my hand while they take blood samples or other little bits of me, since they still don't understand what's going on. She listens to everything; sometimes I wish she'd listen less, because I know what she'll do afterward with what she's learned. It bubbles in her head and spurts out without warning. That's precisely how she went about her suppository suicide attempt. Fifty-seven she gave herself. She got the information in a corridor somewhere in the hospital. She was absolutely delighted to see all the doctors, armed with a whole labyrinth of tubes, digging into her stomach and not finding a thing, and when she's feeling cheerful she still does her imitation of the medics from intensive care who were furious that they couldn't understand what was going on, scolding her to try to find out where the poison had come from or where she had put it. Hah! she replied, very pleased with herself, you're not even warm, looking there! You won't find a thing in my stomach, I put it all up my ass!

But, now that we've moved to another town, the hospital personnel think that my mother is normal, they don't know about her suppository suicide attempt. I keep my mouth shut, they'd be sure to make a huge deal out of it, whereas it is behind her now, at least I'd like to believe it is. But, with the wisdom of my seven years and my twelve septicemias, I can say that it's not over, I'm not even sure that what she's doing to me is even normal. But I won't rebel, I swear I don't know what that really means, anyway. I have to forget the meaning of that word, otherwise I'll get the tourniquet. She wraps it above my knee when I've done something naughty and calls me a lump of caustic potash (because of the potassium). She says that if she waits three hours to remove the tourniquet, I can die right on the spot from a rush of potassium that will cause my heart to burst. So I say, Forgive me, Mommy that I love, and she removes it right away. I've got pins and needles in my leg but she strokes it gently and says that she knows it's painful to be without blood for a while. I know, I know it hurts, she says, rocking me gently.

———

My bouts of septicemia mean that I miss a lot of school, but my mother says at my age it's not serious. She keeps me up to scratch and makes sure I haven't forgotten the letters and shapes and numbers that are on the curriculum. If I have the strength to go back to class between relapses my heart weighs down at seeing my former friends; in any case they keep a safe distance because they heard that my illness means my insides are beginning to rot. I talk about it to my mother and ask her to explain things to them properly, but she says there's nothing she can do to stop them from being mean, it's sheer stupidity. My germs have only one ally, my mother. So I'm actually relieved when I get sick again and can leave the school yard and its vipers for my sickbed and the armchair and my mother's arms. My father's away traveling all the time, particularly when I have relapses. He's afraid of the hospital and he can always find a million things to do elsewhere. Even making babies, says my mother, thinking out loud, when I ask why he hasn't come home. She sleeps curled up in a fetal position in her big bed, and she lets me in with her if I'm having nightmares, holds me close, says that we're better off just the two of us. One summer she'll take me to the Caribbean, but I've got to get some flesh on my bones first. She had to take me out of dance class, so instead between treatments, when I feel up to it, we skip rope, facing each other, and the first one to stop is the loser. I often win, but afterward it takes me a while to get my breath back, so she ventilates me with a machine and says, Breathe, and it's no fun.

I'm lucky because she can sleep with me at the hospital, the nursing staff don't mind because they're swamped, and this way they don't have to keep such close watch over me at night. Mommy takes care of that. She sits on the edge of her bed and when I wake up, feverish, delirious, I never find her asleep, she's always at her post, in a perfect position of intense watch keeping, or sometimes crouched down above a bedpan to do her business, so she doesn't have to leave my side, the toilets are too far away. Then she puts a bit of water into the pot and mixes up a paste; at that point she takes a syringe, attaches the needle, and, calling me her love, inoculates me again with this vile serum, flowing into my body. It's good for you, she says, if she happens to notice my eyes gazing at the syringe as it empties its brown contents into my helpless veins. Go to sleep now, Mommy is here.

# Shame

*It* started up again the day she offered to organize a birthday party for me. She called all the parents to let them know that she'd be there and would keep an eye and make sure we didn't get too close during the slow dances. She promised there'd be no alcohol, and if need be she was prepared to search the bags of anyone she thought might be trying to act clever, or even smell their breath. And if any wanted to sleep over, no problem, she'd set up two dormitories, girls and boys, in separate rooms. As a result I only had seven friends show up, including my godfather's son and his cousin, I didn't know them but Mom invited them, she thought it would be nice to mix up other kids with the usual crowd. She calls it "adding fresh blood." At school quite a few kids were making fun of me: The ban on kisses, even tongueless ones, had created a stir. In the school yard during recess, I don't know how many kids were imitating my mother, I didn't dare try to count. As for my mother, she thought the party was a raging success. After she had promised to stay in the kitchen, out of the way, she eventually set up camp on a chair in the doorway of the living room. She sat tapping her feet in time to the music, and begged my father to ask her to dance but he had some consideration for me and refused. When she couldn't stand it anymore she organized a lady's choice. No one knew what that meant, so she stopped the music to explain, and all the girls invited boys, except that there were more girls than boys, so there were some couples that were just girls and at that point my mother said she didn't want any of that going on in her own home. So my father had to volunteer, like at the puppet show on my fifth birthday. That way there was one more boy. All my guests were sighing—is it any wonder that some young people nowadays end up in a bad way with families like this? At the end of the party I was at the end of my rope and I swore to myself that I would never have anyone over again, ever. Nobody insisted on sleeping over so I cleaned up with my mother, who went on casually dancing in place to the music. My father smiled at me from time to time, a sorry smile, and my mother kept repeating how happy she was about her quiches, and she'd shove the dish under my nose and say, You see, they ate it all! You think only quiche lorraine will cut it but leeks go over just as well!

I may have sworn never to have friends around ever again, but it's sort of pointless to swear things like that, since no one feels like coming over, anyway.

"It's not your fault, but your mother, she's a bit . . ."

"A bit what?"

So as a result I've been visiting my friends at their place. I like other people's mothers, they're normal, they take an interest but from a distance, discreetly, not like mine who's always trying to dream up things for me to do when what I really like is just to hang out. I'm ashamed when she points out that my breasts have grown. I'm ashamed when she wheedles a tiny slice of Gruyère from the cheese vendor for me to eat there on the spot, as if I were three years old, or when she sniffs my hair and asks the pharmacist for something against head odors. I'm ashamed when she shares her opinion on the tuna salad with the checkout clerk or when she yanks at my arm because a bum is lying across the sidewalk. I'm ashamed when she honks the horn, and every time

she says Hello? on the phone, and when she runs, too. I'm
ashamed when she asks friends who phone me to tell her
their last name. I'm ashamed when she chews, or when she
locks herself in the bathroom. I'm ashamed when she says
Honey to my father. I'm ashamed and it's not going to get
any better. Because the real tragedy is that my mother has
offered to accompany my class on the school trip to Rome,
and she has been accepted. And when all the students heard
her name, they went, Oh no, not her. Before we leave I beg
her to keep her mouth shut as much as she possibly can, Always keep it shut, I beg you, Mom. She says I'm impertinent,
and I can see her eyes are moist, so I shut up. I don't dare tell
her to spare me her tanning spray, some wonder she's found
for the summer that makes her legs all ugly brown, as if she
were wearing support hose.

She is keeping watch in the sleeping car. She set up alternate
shifts with the history teacher and the supervisor. She knows
all the risks of rail travel—the madman in the toilets, the
strangler at the bar, the maniac in the corridor. I've already
heard three of my classmates say that my mother is a pain,
only they didn't use the word *pain*, they used a word they'd
be punished for with lines to copy, maybe even entire pages,
if my mother weren't a little hard of hearing. Constance is

the one who pointed out this particular handicap of my mother's. Now the kids say "Choo" every time my mother says "Ah?" and "My French!" every time she says "Pardon?" The worst part is that it makes her laugh, and I really wonder if she's normal. Is she your mother or your grandmother? asked Piotr. I told him he was a filthy Russian, and my mother made me write out forty lines, she wanted to give me more, but she was afraid it might make me vomit, writing in the train. So I copied out "Calling Piotr a filthy Russian is a racist remark, I withdraw it and ask Piotr to please excuse me." When I handed her the page, Piotr called me a stupid bitch, and my mother said, "Ah?" And everyone said, "choo." And then right off she went "Pardon?" And they all went, "My French." She laughed, to show that she knew how to be authoritarian and cool and relaxed at the same time. And she even kissed all the children at bedtime. And she sang a different song for each compartment. She promised to teach us the songs at our evening get-togethers, and I heard one boy say that between now and then her tongue would probably fall off. She appointed a captain for each compartment. She came one last time into mine, and I discreetly asked her to kiss me. She smelled good, with her fresh perfume, and I felt like crying.

———

She's the one who found the youth hostel. She took everything in hand and oversaw the assigning of rooms, letting each of us choose to be with our friends, girls or boys. At one point I heard Jean-Paul say that my mother was better than Miss Tanguy, and that warmed my heart, even if Piotr went on to add that being better than Miss Tanguy was not exactly difficult. Then she asked the director of the youth hostel to prepare us some picnics. We barely had time to get impatient before we were already full, and that was a change from all the trips where you had to wait for hours before you got fed. But I was ashamed again when she unwrapped her sandwich and said, Bon ap! and no one answered her with Petit! So she said it again. To make her stop, and to set the tone, I cried out Petit! and everyone else echoed me, except Icône, who asked what *Petit* meant. Then everyone made fun of Icône and left me alone. But I really wouldn't like for my mother to find out that Icône had an almost intimate sexual relation with Enguerrand. She might want to get involved. So when I see Enguerrand gently caressing Icône's ass just so the others will understand that in the near future they'll be removing the *almost* from *almost intimate*, I distract Mom's attention toward some monument and she's dead pleased that I'm interested in it. For the ones who couldn't care less about art and monuments she makes up stories, promises gelati, and on the whole manages much better than Miss Tanguy—who threatens to give an F to anyone who talks during the tours. Except me, she doesn't dare since I have an accompanying parent. There's one student who's kind of shy, Auguste-Émilien, and spends his time clinging to my mother. She calls him Auguste-M. and that makes him smile, whereas normally he's very solemn. His parents make him wear knickerbockers, so he never looks like everyone else. Mom discreetly showed him how to make cuffs so they'd just look like shorts. And as long as Mom is busy with him, I have all the time in the world to get closer to Luc. He didn't come to my party on the pretext that if he couldn't French with me it wasn't worth coming at all. My girlfriends and I talk a lot about Frenching and Icône knew exactly what it meant. Since then I've been completely obsessed with this kiss that hangs over my head like a promise— or a threat. I've had plenty of training with a poster of James Dean, even if Luc is darker and three-dimensional. At the beginning of the trip, because my mother was there, Luc just ignored me for the most part, but since he noticed that she's busy rehabilitating Auguste-Émilien, he's been coming around more. So I make sure to stick to him at every opportunity so he can't escape. But I'm sad because he's losing interest in me, talking to other girls, often to Chloé, who already has a man in her life, even if she does only see him during vacation when she goes to Saussaie-Les-Pins, and even if she is afraid it will come to an end because of her parents, who just bought a house in Amboise, so now they won't have enough money to keep going to the beach all the time. So there I stand, right next to him, smiling, inhaling his smell when he moves. I walk around to my heart's content, but my heart isn't in it. One evening, as we're finishing our pizza next to some fountain we couldn't care less about now, but we'll care about later on, Mom advises me to keep my distance if I want Luc to like me. She says, Believe me, if you step back from him a little, he'll come running. And she walks off. A little later, she winks at me. I'm ashamed, afraid everyone will think she's got conjunctivitis or something gross like that. But I do what she told me, anyway, and hurry off to sit with a group of girls so she'll stop winking at me. That makes her come back and she tells me to go talk to Antoine. I hate Antoine, but I do as she says. And it works, it all works. Luc goes crazy and can't stop staring at me. My mother winks, and I'm a little bit ashamed, but I smile to her to say thanks.

She taught us the songs she promised. But after a few evenings had gone by we began singing other songs and she liked that, too, unlike Miss Tanguy, who reproached us for making too much racket with our degenerate rhythms. One night Bénédicte was feeling sad and my mother knew just the words to console her and found a phone so that she could call home, even though it isn't allowed during the trip. She got into a discussion with Mr. Maurice, who was against the idea, and she said right out, Would you rather let her cry all night long? And at least three quarters of the kids applauded. The remainder booed Mr. Maurice. When she comes back to check if we're sleeping, I'm ashamed because she's wearing her slippers with the heels, but the kids are mostly looking at her head, at least I hope so. I don't think I'm wrong because I hear Xavier say that my mother has a big nose, and that makes me feel like crying, but in return Luc calls him a dork, and that thrills me. My mother climbs even higher in the polls when she asks that nasty Piotr why his belly is so big and whether he's been going to the toilet regularly since we arrived. Everyone bursts out laughing, and I am really ashamed, but since everyone hates Piotr, who really hurts when he head butts you, everyone praises my mother as awesome and other, even better adjectives.

Our trip is rushing by, we're having a great time, my mother lost her headband leaning over somewhere and we showed her how to replace it with a ribbon, and I really like the way she looks now. I'm still telling a few lies about her, like I quietly tell everyone that she is definitely dying, she's very sick. I get the feeling that might make up for all the times she's ridiculous and I'm ashamed. I tell people about all the misfortunes she's had in life—raped by her father, beaten by her mother, and my father cheating on her. After that I can rest easy as all the students hold her hand and look at her sweetly. On the last night she hands out little presents. She has found a thoughtful little gift to please each of us. She gives us permission to sleep all together, however we like, in the same room.

Luc says he'd like to have a mother like mine, and everyone agrees. Afterward, he kisses me on the mouth, in front of everyone, and I can't remember any of the things I'd planned on doing if this happened, like closing my eyes or putting my arms around his neck, or closing my mouth again once he's finished. I stand there with my mouth gaping open. I don't have anyone around to tell me to close it.

# My Dad's Not a Monster, Mom

*She* is beautiful, leaning over my crib, outside the school, in the car parked on the corner, and then now, twenty years later, in the café where she's waiting for me to drink tea, green tea, it's all the fashion, apparently it can make you lose weight, so she's trying it, you never know—after all, it's about time she lost an actual bone or two. I watched her as she crossed the street, distraught, holding the two sides of her coat together, as if she doesn't want to let herself escape, that vibrant, powerful fear in her guts. I slowed down to let her get there before me, she doesn't like for me to see her, she prefers to be already settled, showing her best side, with the right lighting, if possible. She was once the beauty queen at her school, and with good reason. She has chosen a table toward the back of the café, where she'll feel at ease. In a little bit, we'll go swimming.

She kisses me and the little speck in her eye begins to dance. Before I arrived she had already started keeping time with it, checking, in front, behind, over there, who knows, anything could happen. Some needle might stab her, a blade might fall, and, behind her back, a weapon, a bow is readied. She looks terribly thin when she turns to one side and her dress tightens against her ribs. She wonders where the threat can be coming from, but it is inside her, I know it though she doesn't, not yet, she's searching, the wind could change at any minute. It's like this in the beginning, then she calms down, drinks her tea, the hot water warms her and soothes her, she breathes, here we are, mother and daughter, yes, I had the window repaired, wrote to the insurance company, and the vaccinations are all up to date; yes, the address has been corrected on my ID card. She thinks her hair is limp, she wishes it were thicker so she could wear it long, the way I do, but at her age it seems that short haircuts . . . Anyway, she says, Never mind, your father says it's not bad, but look at my wrinkly neck. I reply that there's no fat, so there can't be any wrinkles, but I'm lying, because I can see tiny lines circling her fine, straight neck like a collar. She finds my sweater very soft, she touches it, wonders if it's new, isn't it rather complicated to take care of, so I tell her I'll give it to her to wash, and she's pleased, at least I think she is. I'll also give her my jacket and my velvet pants, because I'm lousy at taking care of them. She tells me it wouldn't hurt me to try and learn. But I think she does a much better job than I would. In other news, she's debating whether to read a novel a friend of hers told her about, but apparently it's a melodrama and she's afraid she might feel bad afterward. I maintain that it's a rare and good thing to feel upset, she should embrace the opportunity. I ask her for the title, we'll read it together, one after the other, then we can discuss it. She likes the idea. *If I were a little girl, I'd ask you to read it to me sitting by my bedside.*

She's looking at two women her age who are standing in the café, chatting happily, she wonders if she'll have a good time at her goddaughter's wedding on Saturday. She'll get her feet wet, these country weddings in the mud are so annoying. I tell her that it will be good, she'll dance. Then she talks endlessly about the last reception she went to, the bride and groom didn't even thank her for the present—a cake server with a braided handle—and about the registry clerk on the phone who was so unpleasant, she talks about my father, who'll be wearing gray because it's a lovely color.

Yes, things are fine with my boyfriend. She'd like to meet him, she'll make a cake, the one I like best, and we'll drink tea, green tea. Or wine, if we'd prefer, we can even come over for dinner. She'll tell him how as a little girl I invented a father for my doll, who had my father's name. That will annoy me a bit, but Dad will smile at me and shrug his shoulders, as if to say, And so what? Yes, things are fine with my boyfriend, but it might not last. Things are too fine? says Mom with a smile, so you're bored, huh? *Well, yes, even if it's not true, Mom, I am bored. I want to be bored for your sake, the way you are, I want to be bored all day long, except when we have tea.*

My mother coughs, a dry, violent cough, she is holding her sides, and the speck in her eye goes off on tour again, her eye is searching, distraught, for support. I start coughing louder than her, so she stops her furtive searching, with her damp eyes, she stops trembling, she asks me what's going on with this cough, but I'm coughing too hard to reply. Coughing has brought a flush to her cheeks, she smiles and pours me some water, she strokes my fingers. You're choking, she says. No. She thinks it's a bad idea to go swimming in such a state. Are you sure you don't smoke, you promise me?

But I insist, we said we would, we're going swimming. She thinks my pool bag is fun, she looks at it, lifts it up by each corner, weighs it, says it's awfully heavy for my back. She holds my arm, we stop outside a shop window, there's a skirt she likes, the speck has stopped roaming, suddenly Mom is quite content, she's been dreaming about this skirt, low-waisted, with pleats at the bottom, in a gauzy material, so we go in, but the speck is back; besides, it's so complicated, trying to talk to the salesgirl. *I'll talk to her if you want.* But the skirt's no good, it's too short, at her age it looks ridiculous, *stop that business about your age.* And then the salesgirl isn't taking care of her. She's answering another customer's questions at the same time. She says, Come on, let's go, it didn't suit me, anyway.

We're swimming in parallel lanes, and as soon as I'm about to overtake her I slow down, I want to let her beat me, like before, on vacation, when I was little and I would scold her for winning. I'm breathing like an ox, I tell her I can't take any more of these laps, it's exhausting, and I cling to the edge while she keeps going back and forth building all that muscle tone, proud she can swim so much longer than I can. She turns on her back, stretches her arms far behind her.

When she stops, I wish she would start again, so I ask her to show me how to swim straight when you're on your back, she explains the method, her speck is sleeping, she tells me to join her, to do like her. *I am doing like you but not as well.* So you see, reach your arms straight behind you and leave your ears in the water, under water, don't lift your head out of the water, you have to hear your breathing, now you hear? *No, Mom, I don't hear anything.* There are little broken veins around her knees, and behind her ankles, veins that have been almost imperceptibly ruined, like tiny little injuries, gathered there, and that weigh just enough to slow her down, with each stroke. It's not a big deal, no great torment, and meanwhile the wind in her head never leaves her any peace. Since I left home she just sees time going by and doesn't know what's left to do. She often tells my father that in ten years it will be over. Everything. Them. Life. Just to make her cry, he asks her why it will be ten years from now, maybe it could happen right this minute.

The speck in her eye has replaced the sparkle. Once again my mother has shut down, prey to her anxiety—what can she do? She's bored, she wearies easily, she worries when the speck comes and blurs her vision, she says her retina is becoming detached. In the changing room she talks about multiple sclerosis, a tumor on the spinal column, a dislocated shoulder—yes, these can sometimes affect your vision. She swears it's true. And I can't disagree in cases like this, it would be too brutal. The only way to make her happy is to come up with something even worse. *Unless it's a brain tumor, Mom.* And at that she smiles, she'll have something to fight against. After all, I saw her laps, I'm a witness, the struggle has begun, she won't give up.

"You know about your father?" my mother says as we leave the changing rooms.

Yes, I know he's cheating on you, but he's not a monster. I know he fell in love with a thirty-year-old girl, that the trip to Germany was actually in Italy. I know she was there when they handed out the trophies, you were wearing a yellow dress and she was looking at you, she had a scarf in her hair and a dark look. Yes, I know it's over, but she's the one who left. *My dad isn't a monster, Mom.*

"So you know?" she asks. "Can't you guess? Try, please."

And the speck is back, there's no relief from it. We're walking along the street, she's clinging to my arm, she asks me if I'd like to go and have a drink before we each go home.

"Guess! Come on!" says my mother as she begins to cry.

"I don't understand," I say, "don't cry, it's not serious."

She nods, the speck falls. She says she's happy, it's just all this emotion . . . She goes on:

"What do you suppose I've found for your father for his birthday? What do you think he would like for his birthday—a man like him who has everything?"

And more. She's leaving him. She's going away. She's leaving with her head held high, and the fear inside, she's going to leave her place, that's enough, she thinks that's enough. And I'm just as bad, I covered for my Dad, but it was for her sake, I did it for her, I thought I could spare her, what would have happened this summer if I had shown her where his lover was living, in the same town as us, the little hotel on the corner, just a stone's throw from our house, where he went to love, instead of going for a walk. We often had to wait for him, remember, Mom, and you said, That's fine, he unwinds in the summer. *I wanted to hold you close enough that you wouldn't see, but you saw, didn't you?*

I don't want her to tell me she's going to leave Dad or anything like that, I don't want it to fall apart between them now that I'm gone, the house needs them to stay together or else the walls will collapse, we have to get them back together again, maybe an accident would help, I've had enough of life always smiling on me and sneering at her. The speck comes out of her eye, lands on my cheek like a fly, I chase it away, slap myself. And my mother, astonished, watches as I slap myself. She suddenly seems fine.

I've got to go, I'm leaving, she tells me to wait for her, No, I'm already really late, But give me a chance to tell you! She hurries behind me. *Oh no, please don't tell me.* But then you knew when girls were calling and I was protecting him, protecting him or you, I don't know, I'd go and get him very quietly, and as if nothing were going on I'd say, It's for you, it's work. And you were in the kitchen, and you'd reply that really, what sort of funny hours did they keep, to be disturbing my father like that. I put music on so you wouldn't hear him say to those girls, Let's meet, or, I've been thinking about you.

She catches up with me and asks what's gotten into me, where am I running off to like that? What do you mean? I'm walking normally, I have to go, Mom. Let me tell you, come on, *No, no, don't tell me anything,* yes, the cleaning woman, that time, in the hall, just his hand, maybe, but he took her by the waist, I saw him and I came over to you so you wouldn't move. I kiss her quickly on the cheek and rush off at full tilt, she shouts even louder, shouts through her smile,

"We're going to sleep at the lighthouse! I have the authorization! He'll be pleased, don't you think? I've been wanting that authorization for so long. We're going to sleep in the lighthouse, both of us, all the way at the top!"

The speck splats against my forehead, my mother is running right behind me. I don't want to give it back to her, she's going to the lighthouse, all alone with my father, without her speck, and now it's gone into my ear. They're going to stay together, life is going to keep them together, they won't leave each other. There are some events that bring parents closer. You just have to find them.

Just as she's about to catch up with me, I cross without looking.

# Punching Bag

*I don't* understand why my daughter is so violent. I tried to get an appointment with a support group to talk about it, but they can't see me until two months from now. I get the feeling a lot of mothers have a problem with authority. While I wait for them to find me a therapist, they've offered me a course that has nothing to do with my problems, but the counselor thinks that a discussion with other women who are having a rough time of it would be good for me. So I agreed to take part in the session titled "Women: Find your punch so men will stop punching you." It's free and it will mean that I won't have to spend that time in my daughter's company, since I've become her slave as of late. Her father left me for an older, unemployed woman, go figure, especially as the wretched woman already has three children and two dogs. My daughter likes her a lot, she thinks she bakes good cakes.

After we split up, everything would have been fine if my daughter hadn't instantly turned into a war machine. I didn't want to rush her, because of the separation. In the beginning I thought she was having a hard time because of her father's absence and was making me pay. Her grades plummeted, she claimed she had headaches and stomach cramps so she could hang around at home rather than go to class, she watched a lot of television and I didn't criticize her, even though her blasting music was driving me nuts. I let her live through her crisis while I finished my mourning. After all, it was me her father left. Certainly before he left her. And then one day I decided to take control of the house again, everything was going to the dogs, above all her bedroom, which she forbade me from entering from that day on.

"Tidy it up if you don't want me to. I understand that you want to have your own territory, but show some respect for it."

"What the fuck do you care?"

I read a lot of magazines where they tell you how to deal

with kids who are going through a crisis, so I decided to apply all their advice to the letter.

"Listen, sweetheart, I'm not your enemy. I was a teenager myself once. Right now you're going through a difficult period. However" (in the magazine the journalist had insisted on the importance of using connecting words between thoughts, as essential as the hinges on a door, to make the young person understand and accept the logic behind an adult's thoughts), "we are living under the same roof, and you are duty-bound to follow certain rules, such as politeness and . . ." (I'd forgotten the rest). "I want you to clean your room, it stinks."

"You have no business giving me orders. I'm in my own house."

"You are in your own house, but you are also in my house. How would you feel if I left my things lying around all over the place?"

"Who gives a shit."

"Listen, I'll make it simple. Let's make a deal. You can try to act cheerfully and agree to go along with the few rules of the house, or else there will have to be punishments. I can impose some rules of my own, too, you know."

"Go ahead and try, you old bag."

———

I don't recall the magazine giving any advice on how to deal with these kinds of insults. I tried to put myself in the shoes of the journalist, who was obviously better informed than I am, and as quickly as I could, I retorted:

"You old what?"

"You old bag! Slut! Bitch!"

She stomped off to her room, and I was fine with that because it is no doubt what I would have told her to do, but in the article they suggested using this punishment for kids under twelve, and my daughter is nearly sixteen. I decided to eat alone across from her empty chair, I sat thinking a lot as I stared at this spot where I'd watched her grow up. But, overcome by nostalgia, I finally switched on the radio. That's when I heard a mother talking about how her child hit her. I burst out laughing, wondering how people could put up with stuff like that so casually. At just that point my daughter came into the kitchen, opened the fridge, and took out the foie gras that I had bought ahead of time for her birthday.

"Put that foie gras back in the fridge, please, it's not for today."

"It's for my birthday, right? So it's mine, right? So I'm going to eat it, and you can just shut up. You don't actually think I'd spend my birthday with you, do you?"

"Put that foie gras back where it belongs and you go back to your room. I don't want to see you this evening."

"That works fine, I don't want to see you, either!"

She left the kitchen and went to flop onto the sofa in the living room with her foie gras. I didn't have a clue what to do next, but I could tell I was beginning to lose my temper, that I might even lose it altogether. I decided to deal with it as I felt best and forget about the journalist's advice, who had really let me down where extreme cases were concerned. I went into the living room, switched off the television, my daughter switched it right back on, and I stood in front of it to hear her ask me if I thought I was a freaking window, so I grabbed the foie gras from her and pointed my finger in the direction of her room. She picked up a vase and smashed it on the floor. I called her hysterical, she began hurling insults at me and rushed off to her room, slamming the door. I had won.

The respite did not last long, she came back out, her butt barely covered by a scarf, her Barbie duffel bag slung over her shoulder, she opened the door, and then was gone. I was a sorry sight with that foie gras in my hand, in my nose the scent of vanilla musk, that could always be of use if I needed her followed, well, if it doesn't nauseate the dogs too much. I filled a pan with water, and when she walked out of the building I dumped it on her head. She was so surprised that it gave me time to run downstairs to force her to come back up. I yanked her by the arm, she fought me off, she said she was going to kill me. The water had made her perfume even stronger. In my soul I felt like a true adolescent and I replied, Over my dead body.

In the days that followed, our interactions grew steadily worse, so I just decided to let her do as she wanted, and it seemed to work, things got better. We were able to live together. One day when she wasn't there I tidied up her room, I didn't throw out much except for some old Kleenex and trash, didn't read any of the papers that were lying around, but when she came home, she threw herself at me. She hit me.

And now here I am in the circle of those who cry, "Find your punch so men will stop punching you." All the women here have been beaten by their spouses. I feel embarrassed to have to tell them that in my home it's my daughter who's the aggressor. Each of them has an opinion about my situation.

"Send her to boarding school."

"Talk to her father."

"Hit her harder than she hits you."

"Stop feeding her, she'll lose her strength."

All these women harassed by their spouses seem overwhelmed by my life story. One of them points out a specific aspect of my personality, says I'm too accommodating, and then, afraid she might have offended me, touches my arm and says, Listen, you don't realize it.

Well that does me a whole lot of good. She can even write it on my cast, but it won't help the fact that yesterday my daughter broke my nose. I was vacuuming in the living room, she unplugged the vacuum because the noise was bothering her, which I can understand, and I didn't even try to switch it back on, I figured I'd vacuum the next day, so I just left it there.

"Aren't you going to put it away?" she said.

"Nah, I just have to get it out again tomorrow, anyway."

"Put it away. Stop leaving your stuff lying around."

I smiled, I thought she was mimicking me and that this was a joke. And then, she told me that I had such a stupid look on my face that it would be better if I couldn't make any face at all, and she punched me in the nose. It started bleeding immediately, I rushed off to the emergency room and as she was pouring a bucket of water on my head she shouted out the window that she hoped I'd bring George Clooney home with me.

The group nods then shakes their heads, yes, no. I insist that, unlike them, I do not want to flee my home. I like my house, and I don't want to end up in some center with an assumed identity, wearing a wig or dyeing my hair. I have every intention of going home, even if I lose an eye or my other arm. As for my sense of smell, given my daughter's persistent taste for heady, sugary notes, I don't miss it. Thanks to my support group I understand that if I combine dialogue with action I should finally be able to get somewhere. I wait until we've finished dinner, which has been spent in front of the television, and then, not daring to switch it off, I begin to speak. I forge right ahead, thinking of what Anne-Valérie, my team partner, said, and hearing her voice in my head: Go for it. She'll call me soon to check that I've followed through.

"Do you want to go to boarding school?" I say to my daughter, lowering my voice.

"What's with you, already? Don't talk to me."

"I'm thinking of enrolling you in boarding school next fall, I'm not sure we can continue to live together. But I'll find a nice place, somewhere out in the country, would you like that?"

"I'd prefer Tahiti. Go on, leave me alone, I said."

And on that note she gets up and shakes my chair. I don't think she means to knock me to the floor but, with my arm in a cast, I lose my balance and fall against the stove, landing hard on the elbow of my good arm and I scream. So she tells me to shut up and locks herself in her room.

With both my arms in a cast, I don't know how to get to my discussion group anymore, and I wonder if it wouldn't be a good idea to learn how to punch. It's weird, but I'm beginning to be afraid out in the street. So I close the shutters and lock the doors. This has been going on for a month. When I hear my daughter's key in the lock, I race to my room, even at the risk of hurting myself again. I fix dinner and leave everything on the kitchen table. I figure that, like with wild animals, you mustn't let her get hungry. When I can hear that she's finished, I go and clean up, or sometimes I don't, I stay in my room, sitting on the armchair that I've pushed against the door to keep it shut. She slams her door, opens it, slams it again, that's her latest kick. I can hear the upstairs neighbor banging with a broomstick against the floor, but there's nothing I can do, except maybe call him to ask him to come down here and rescue me.

———

"Come out of there, I need you!" shouts my daughter one afternoon when she was meant to be at school.

"I'm resting. What do you want?" I say, through the door. I try to keep my voice dignified, normal, but take a step backward and protect my face.

"Fix the hem on my pants, I'm going out tonight."

"Slide them under the door! I'll fix them later."

"They won't fit under the door, bitch!"

"Leave them outside, I'll get them, did you pin them for me?"

"No. I'm wearing them. You're going to do it."

This business of hemming her pants reassures me that she needs a mother who is more or less functioning. I open the door, don't meet her eyes but look at the bottom of her pants, and her new boots: cowboy boots with metal tips. I squat down. How I would like to plant the pins all round her ankles, I'd like her to bleed, to drain away, to vanish, yes, I would like to eat her and vomit her back out afterward, or put her boots on and give her a few good kicks. She crushes her cigarette butt on the floor, then kicks it a bit further away with the toe of her boot. I carry on with my pinning. Then she spits a few inches from my fingers.

"By the way, I'm going to live with Dad."

"That's nice."

"You don't care?"

"Yes, yes."

"No, you don't, you don't care."

That's not exactly true. And it's not just that I don't not care, I am overcome with joy. But how can I say so without her clobbering me for the umpteenth time, since it would involve confessing to something she clearly will not appreciate. Anne-Valérie comes to mind, Anne-Valérie who no longer calls me, because I begged her not to, and it was part of our agreement to give up on the other person if she could no longer meet the challenge, but I think of her all the same, she warms my thoughts and burns my tongue, like a dazzling ray of sunlight. And suddenly, before I realize what I am doing, I say:

"No, I don't care, I'm even delighted. As for your boots, they are absolutely every bit as distinguished as your stepmother. I hope that her dogs will poop in them and I am asking you to leave now."

"After my hem."

"You've put on weight. You have a fat ass. Go on, big butt, get out."

"Start sewing, you old bag."

So I stand up, despite both arms in a cast, and I spit in

her face. She looks down so that I won't see my saliva flowing like some huge tear across her cheek. She leaves and her pants are dragging along the ground, hiding her boots. I figure that a few yards down the road she'll trip and fall into her new life without even needing me to push her.

# Knots and Nuts

*There's* a tree, and a rabbit hole. The rabbit comes out of the tree, no, the hole, goes around the hole, no, the tree, goes around the tree, and then goes back into his hole, you see? A story for each knot, that's how sailors do it, and in life, too, the knot is in the story.

My mother dreams of a knot, the way others dream of a child, a man, or a journey. She opens the package, she is waiting for a present, then what a disappointment, so, without giving up hope, she starts over, holds on, holds to her belief, She'll get there, she says to Madame Hervé, who comes sometimes to see if I'm making progress. It's like with the dish-towel folding, she mustn't give up hope, I'll figure it out, for ten years she's been showing me and soon

I'll be able to make a rectangle. I sweep, I hang up my coat, I can mix the pie dough, brush the dog, I can get dressed all by myself, but my mother's the one who chooses my clothes, she doesn't like my flowery style. I know how to start the cassette of *The Sound of Music* and lock the door. My mother told Madame Hervé that since she hasn't been able to tame my imbecile brain, she's got my hands used to doing a few tasks that are indispensable if you want to be on good terms with the house you live in. I won't have a husband, but that mustn't stop me from knowing how to make my bed. Since I got a comforter things are better. It was one of Madame Hervé's ideas, she's used to children who are dummies. I had a real problem with sheets, and my mother would shout at me to pull on the fitted sheet. She insisted that you had to stretch the blanket tight over the bed and then fold the top sheet back over it—insisted so often, in fact, that my brain just shut down and folded itself up in a little corner of my head. And then there was the problem of the corners at the end of the bed, she swore again, over my dead body, that until I could learn to do them correctly I wouldn't budge from there, she shouted so much that I couldn't go to bed, they had to teach me all over how to go to sleep, I didn't know anymore which way I was supposed to lie down so I would stand for hours on the bed facing the wall acting like an orchestra conductor to the waves of wallpaper that turn into mice if you stare at them long enough. Then they run away.

My brain goes on vacation, takes a rest, nothing I can do about it, but my mother wonders if one day I'll stop chasing flies. Often she just gives in, you can't make a cake with rotten eggs or go very far in a leaky hot-air balloony, balloony, balloony.

Standing on the bed, facing the wall, I open my mouth, and invite a wave of paper to play with my tongue, I've already seen mouths pressed together and I think I'm old enough to suck face. A salty taste enters my mouth, disturbs me, enthralls me. The trouble is that when I start to feel something, I need to go pee.

My mother puts her fingers inside my mouth, shoves the mush in. Don't move, you piss like an animal, now you'll eat like an animal. I squeeze my hands around her wrists. Keeping time, she bangs my head against the damp bread in the dog bowl. She leans over me and stops me from moving. Horrible wretch, she says, loosening her grip, don't count on me, don't ever count on me again—it's one thing if you piss while you're asleep, but wide awake? What's getting into you?

She falls to the ground and cries for a long time, her head in her hands, strands of hair caught between her fingers. She drags herself along the tiles. She is torn between her desire to tear me to pieces and the fear, always there, that she might kill me. She'd like to keep me alive, for the times when having me around keeps her busy, for those blissful days when she takes my photo after dressing me up, with eye masks and hats with veils and motorcycle helmets or firemen's helmets, those are the good days, to make up for the bad ones. She perseveres, there must be some things that I'll end up learning, okay—with the bicycle, it was unreasonable to expect she could remove the training wheels, but something else, just some sort of useful movement that I could turn into an occupation. As for my chewed-up hands—she is as ashamed of them as she is of my laugh or my flabby face. She wants my hands to stop waving around for nothing. She gives me baths when the sun goes down, the hour when everything oppresses her so deeply that she draws two baths just to pass the time. During the first bath she washes me and scrubs so hard you'd think I was covered in soot. During the second, she puts a bath mitt on my hands and shows me how to rub. I sort of manage, she's pleased. It's a celebration when she has won, so I clap my hands together, I congratulate myself, bravo, Mommy, and she shouts, blinded with soap, don't do that, you can't do that. When she looks at me she is counting, but I don't know what. Twenty years I've been alive, and she doesn't know how it's happened or why.

She feels bad that she hit me, I like it when she feels bad. I go out quietly, wiping my mouth. The dog licks my fingers. I take him with me and close my bedroom door. He sniffs my wet behind. I sit on the bed, the scene of my crime, I take off my pajamas and put them on the edge of a chair the way I've seen my mother do, they'll dry. I put on my pink dress, she will love me. Every morning she hopes some feeling for me will come to her, some feeling hidden in the air or in the shadows, something you could just pluck or gather delicately from the clouds. But every morning she finds only despair. I ate the socks she put on my hands because she would like my hands, at least my hands, just that, two hands, some fingers, she begs for God's mercy, she would like for my hands not to become stumps during the night, what is she going to do with me? I ate the socks—you could call them mittens— and my fingers wiggle, exposed, peeled, spotted with blood. I eat my hands, the only way I've found to stop my hands is with my teeth. My mother says I'm already complicated enough, already twisted and weird and inadequate enough and meanwhile no, that's still not enough, I have to go and ruin my hands. What's the point of having the hands of a pianist when my brain can't remember the name of one single note? So I chew my nails, my skin, and sometimes even deeper into my finger, whole pieces of myself. Abscesses start growing, I hide them under my dollies. But my hands keep fluttering, as if to chase my mother away.

My mother's lips always shine after an argument, as if someone has been drooling on her. She waits for a long time before coming into my bedroom, but mental retards don't have a very precise notion of time, let alone how much has passed. She comes in, I put my hands together, order them to stay still, one inside the other; if she sees them going crazy, these flyswatters of mine, she'll get mad, whereas she's just found a way to stay calm, and this despite the advice of Madame Hervé who, where the urinary issue is concerned, is against infantilizing retards.

"We're going out. Stick this on."

She tosses a diaper onto my bed and goes back out, slamming the door. It's long and rectangular, no elastic, and it sticks out on either side of my underpants. She opens the door again.

"And take that dress off. Put on your yellow pants. Then close your mouth, put on a barrette, stand up straight, take your fingers out of your nose, don't stare at people, don't touch children, don't jump, don't shout, stay dignified, don't clap when you see policemen, do you understand? You don't put your hand in your underpants. If you put your hand in your panties, I warn you . . . You put your hands away, in your pockets, understand? Control yourself. You're torturing me."

"I want my dress."

Out in the street, she takes me by the hand. When she's holding one of my hands, that stops me from hunting with both of them, so the solitary one still goes after the flies, but you don't notice it as much. My mother hopes that some-day she'll be able to let go of my hand, that it will become autonomous, so she's organizing exercises. She squeezes it harder and harder, then tosses it to one side. I grab the bottom of her sleeve to have something to hold to, without touching her skin so I don't annoy her, but she breaks free with a shrug of her shoulders, moving her handbag. I have to control her. I know it is time to let her go ahead of me. If I walk in front, she reproaches me for all the comments that flow in my wake.

"I told you to take off that dress, everybody's making fun of you, it's a costume, understand? People don't go out dressed like that. You're a big girl. You must act dignified.

Don't forget that your hands already don't help you look particularly normal. Learn to control yourself."

"Yes. Morgan le Fay."

Thanks to me, men turn around to look at her. She ought to be grateful, but no, she sways her hips, dragging behind her this piss bag who is careful not to crush her beautiful shadow, though in actual fact I really would like to jump on it with both feet together. My crazy hands are clutching at the air left and right, the more I hold them back, the more they dance. So my mother reaches out her hand to me again, I grab it in passing and we cross the street, we're walking past the bakeries, she asks me to stop staring at the cakes like that. We make a systematic detour to avoid going by Marinette's cart, because my mother doesn't like it when I say hello to Marinette. Apparently I don't say hello normally and it's embarrassing. It's about time I learned to train my voice. When I'm hungry, I lick my mother's arm, from her elbow to her wrist, it makes her scream. To make me stop she takes a snack out of her bag. She's put some chocolate into a bread roll, I'm happy. Normally she puts butter, a thick layer, she says I'm lucky to have a mother who remembers my calcium and worries about speeding the regrowth of the skin on my fingers. After I've eaten my snack, I have to put my hands under my bottom and wait for her on the park bench, she won't be long. She just has an appointment with Patrick Lamy. She has to leave me.

I look at the calcium-deficient children playing in the sand. I spread my legs a little so that the scotch tape from the wee-wee diaper won't rub against my skin. She spreads her legs, too, with Patrick Lamy, and she'll for sure have some children like the ones playing here. I give the bread to the pigeons, I munch on the chocolate, I think about my dog, I wonder why Mommy doesn't want me to stay at home with him. I like my dog. When I play with my hands, he gives me his paw or lies down with his chin on the floor, as if my waving fingers were concocting him some nice dessert. Night is falling. The children are starting to go home, I pick up a lost toy, I put it under my bottom and I wait for my mother to come back, her mouth all bitten, her body all wobbly, her throat hoarse, flushed with love. She'll be going to Marseille soon with Patrick Lamy, he's a navy fireman. She's going to talk with Madame Hervé to see if she can find me a good home, because she's afraid that in Marseille I might feel a bit lost. I'll be able to go there if I have vacation. There are volunteer chaperones who take retards down there in a train, in a car, and in silence.

In the square the mothers go on talking and keep an eye on the games of the last children. Sometimes they hold a big rubber band with their feet or keep score during a competition on the slide. I'm the biggest kid on the square, I keep an eye on things, I act as if I was in charge of some kid in the sandbox, I pick one at random and give him a silly smile the minute he looks my way. Half the time he sticks his tongue out. With my left hand gone to sleep from the weight of my body and my right hand shoved into my mouth I watch the children clinging to their mothers, night is falling, they're sad. They button their coats, clean off their hands, full of dirt from playing on the ground. They leave and the lovers arrive. Classes have just let out from the local high school, everyone's kissing, there are little moans from the grass. I put my feet on the bench to look a bit saucy, I figure that's better than looking retarded. I keep a look out for the mice who come after the kisses. I rub my bottom against the wooden bench while I wait for my mother and I grind my teeth together as if I were rubbing two flints. A little flickering flame, a great moving terror, here she comes at a run, slowed by her pointy heels, her hair all disheveled and her face damp from Patrick Lamy's kisses. I go toward her, she opens her arms, holds me close for a second, then complains that she's hot and sticky. And then she says, Come, come on, we're going to take a bath, we'll make knots, you remember, knots of all sorts, wonderful knots. She hurries me along, she wants us to get home, she says we're going to eat some pasta, pack our suitcases, and make knots. After the bath she explains to me that ten days isn't a very long time, we have to enjoy each other's company, but how long is ten days? It's the time between my name day and my birthday, but what is my name? It's a bit more than the gap of one week between two balancing workshops but a little less than the time that goes by between two appointments at the speech therapist's. The last time we were there, ten days ago, is when Patrick Lamy asked Mommy to go and live with him, but without me. I was behind the door, but I heard, I'm not deaf. She didn't hesitate.

The police are wondering whether my mother didn't try to stop herself falling at the last minute by grabbing the banister of the stairwell below the place where the rope strangled her, it's hard to explain why her hand is closed so tight around the railing. It was the girl who found her, she grabbed her by her feet to make her move, say the police. I nod, they smile at me. What I don't tell them is that my mother's body spiraled first in one direction and then spun at great speed in the other. I grabbed her by the ankles, one ankle in each hand, my hands were busy for once, and I added to the momentum, first in one direction and then the other, I made my mother waltz this way and that, yes, I am her executioner. And I clapped my hands, over and over, beneath her hanging body. The knot around her neck didn't give a millimeter, I've mastered my knots. Just before she got stiff she said something, but I didn't understand, I think it was, Let me go, or maybe, Please, I beg you.

We'll take good care of you, said Madame Hervé who drove me to the center. Your mother couldn't stand her life anymore, but it's not your fault.

The center is a paradise for hands. On Wednesdays we have a Chinese shadow puppet workshop. An expert shows us how to arrange our fingers to make decorations on the walls. With Rose and Emilie we paint our nails, and we haven't given up on the idea that someday we'll find a way to make shadow puppets in color.

When Madame Hervé takes me out for a walk and then I come back, or when I sit by the window in this nuthouse to look out and see what the weather is like or what nature's up to, all the others, in the garden, with their dozens of hands,

wave to me. Their palms are soft like the inside of bunnies'
ears, just like the ones in Patrick Lamy's garden, the ones he
described to my mother, my mother who won't be going
anywhere. See, in Marseille, too, there is a rabbit hole, with
a tree, the rabbit comes out of the hole, goes around the tree,
and then goes back into the hole.

# My Mother Never Dies

*No,* Doctor, Mother is fine. It's typical of certain people to let themselves go a bit, especially in summer. Everyone's hot, everyone's tired, you have to make a huge effort—take a good shower, go out into the fresh air and get over it. I know I'm not as old as she is, there's no reason for you to point that out to me. It's getting really difficult and just because my daughter loves her grandmother doesn't give her the right to criticize everything I do. She doesn't like the way I talk to her, she says that I'm always admonishing her—for once she used a new word—and she doesn't like it, but if no one takes charge, my mother is going to founder, so she uses the attention we pay her in order not to lift one little finger. It's not doing her any favors. If we do everything before she has a chance to do it herself, she will wither away. Yes, I do force her, but it's not to annoy her, it's to get her going. The other day she left the gas on again and didn't even drink the water she'd been boiling. All she had to say in reply was that she couldn't find the matches. But the matches were right there. At Christmas we even gave her a dispenser for matches that we hung on the wall. We explained carefully to her what it was, we showed her how to use it, but no, it's just like with the microwave, in one ear, out the other. You know what I think? It's some sort of blackmail, so that we'll be there all the time. The proof is that whenever I get her a nurse, she sulks. It's embarrassing. She just gazes out the window. I can't spend all my time over there, I have a life, too.

One time I got there and found her bent over her checkbook as if it were the source of some despair. She'd signed where you put the date, and put the year where you put the amount. I tore up the check, she asked me to fill it out for her, I refused, and I waited for her to finish the job that she's supposed to do, and do it all, by herself. She was trembling on purpose, writing utterly illegibly. I made her do it over, anyway. Twice. She began to cry. And my daughter, who was with me, gave me a sharp look, what business is it of hers anyway, she's *my* mother. If everything I do is all wrong, maybe I should leave the two of them alone there one day, and go fly my kite somewhere else, as my daughter so amiably told me. I know what is good for my mother, and the less she does, the less she will do. It's like with her sleep, if she sleeps too much then she's groggy all day. Make her wake her up, Doctor, why don't you! Let her take her two-hour siesta, that should be enough, already. I call her to tell her to close her eyes, and then I come personally to rouse her at around three thirty. But when she sleeps till after six, that's really letting things slide. And you should see the way she eats her afternoon snack. I do buy her the butter short-bread cookies that she likes, but she goes and makes such a spectacle of herself. She gets crumbs all over, and I even have to wipe the corners of her mouth. She doesn't even say thanks when I bring her the tray. Half the time she spills the tea. She doesn't notice it, or pretends not to; she leaves her sheets full of spots and puddles. So I get her up, I wipe off the wrist that's all red from the scalding, I try not to shout, but she's so irritating that, yes, from time to time I do tell her I'm fed up with her never paying any attention. And I yank her arm to get her to stand up. One time she said, You're hurting me, and I couldn't let go of her, it really paralyzed me, I have a heart, but I don't like having my leg pulled. We're having trouble getting her up today! She's fast asleep, huh! Sleeps pretty soundly for someone who's been traumatized!

She may be tired some of the time, but I can hardly believe that she's tired all the time. She taught me not to lie and now she's the one mocking me. She doesn't even make an effort with the easy stuff, like television programs. I try to get her to talk about some new show, and she has a mental block, she says she doesn't remember. Well, that's not my mother, my mother is not some senile old wreck. You know, Doctor, I'd like to thank you for your kindness in coming here, I don't know what she tells you, but I'm not a mean person, I try to be here like the stake supporting a branch that's gotten sort of lazy and tends to droop. I know we already talked about how she lets herself go, but I didn't tell you about what she gets up to on the telephone, when the children call her and sometimes she doesn't recognize them. She can spend ten minutes answering just yes or no, I don't what they've done to her in that place, but it's not depression, she's playing some really wicked game, you can't fool me. I'm right, aren't I, Doctor? Ever since I hired this nurse so I could have some time to myself, my mother's been blackmailing me, that's the word for it and no other. When I talk to her she closes her eyes, very pleasant, I assure you.

Will you have a cup of coffee, Doctor? And instead of help-ing me when she comes along, my daughter scolds me as if *she* were my mother. Because my own mother, yes, she did scold me from time to time, though I'd be happy now if she were to reclaim some of her rights, but no, she just lets people talk and lets things go, just like her back—the way she slumps in her chair! Sit up straight, I say. She can't! shouts my daughter, why are you bugging her?

That time I was really pleased, my mother told my daughter not to speak to me like that, so I felt somewhat calmer. It's driving me crazy, Doctor, you have to do some-thing, give her some vitamins, pick her up and shake her, if we keep on feeling sorry for her things will really get out of hand.

Yes, Doctor, I have all the results, and apart from a few papers I haven't opened, everything looks normal, even her cholesterol. I don't know where I left the blood counts, but it's okay, it's just a passing fatigue. For about a year, maybe. Are you aware of anything? Do you think if I try to take her to the sea this year? But it's tricky getting her into the car, she can't move well anymore.

No, Doctor, my mother is not going to die.

———

Here we really are on the verge of hysteria, and all anyone, all of them, can find to do is criticize my actions. I hope you're not about to start, too, Doctor? I'd like to see how you'd manage if you had a mother who drools.

You've got it wrong, Doctor, I tell you she has to stand up. So why are you closing her eyes?

# Ten Operations in Ten Years

*I am* walking, and as long as I take my time, she stays. She told me she'd wait for me before she died, she said it just like that, the words in that order, calmly, with composure, and she always keeps her word. It's the way she is, for my sake. If I had taken the car and arrived by now, she would already be gone. I know the deal. I call her several times a day. She picks up, she's never too tired to speak to me, she says nothing about herself, she asks how far I've gone. All she says is Hurry. I tell her that my feet have not yet finished snuffing out the light of the sun.

Sometimes she wakes up and calls me. One night, the phone rang and it was her on the line, informing me that she was about to die. Soon, she said; when, she couldn't say exactly, but soon, that's a promise. I told her I was going to come, she said, Yes, several times, as if there were already an echo. But on foot, I added, I want to come on foot. Echoes rebounding, we fell silent. I live in the south, with its virgin, deserted hills, a wilderness; she lives in Paris, she is from a family that has been Parisian for three generations, and so what. Soon. She wanted to see me, but said nothing, forced nothing, just repeated, Do as you like, as you wish, whatever you think. There was a note of regret in her voice, as if she didn't understand, a doubt. I called her back to tell her she'd see me again. In any event I'll wait for you, she said again.

I am walking to my mother, counting my steps, the churches, the pebbles. I have eight hundred kilometers ahead of me, and then some if I decide to go around the villages, besides I've never been to Velaux, or to Les Guigues. And what about Les Cravons?

I don't understand what my responsibility is in this thing, with this date, ending the game, I don't understand why my mother can't just wait some more—weeks, nine, months, nine, years, nine, even more, to do this, to set out, to pursue it, to finish. There's a particular image of her that often comes to me. I was a child. She had put on lipstick before

I got to the hospital, she had just had an operation, she was wearing a kimono in shades of green, she was smiling, seated, leaning slightly back against the pillows, wiggling her toes. She didn't tell me about her operation, I talked to her about school, where everything was going wrong, but I didn't tell her that. I told her it was fine, my grades, friends, sports, recess. Sometimes you say *it's fine* and it sounds like the way you say *that's enough*. She stayed at the hospital for a very long time. They told me not to worry, but then they said, Ten operations in ten years, can you imagine? Suddenly it seemed they'd said too much, so then they explained that it was nothing. Oh good, so much the better, I thought, ten years, right from the moment I was born, can you imagine? My father would wake me in the morning to go to school, in the evening he'd take me to Ferrari's, an Italian restaurant in a basement with a shop at street level and vegetables in jars watching us as if through a porthole as we left. I would convert the figures: ten operations in ten years, eight in eight years? Perhaps. Or why not all of them the same year? But in that case you wouldn't say ten years, you'd be happy with one year, you'd say ten operations in one year, and my father would stop, but no, he keeps going, insisting, going deeper, getting her in deeper, getting us in deeper, he tells my teacher, the dance teacher, the speech therapist, ten operations in ten years, how can you not lose everything, when we spend so much time opening up my mother.

And to her friends she says: ten operations in ten years. Oh really, and how old is your little girl? Ten. It never stops. Twenty operations in twenty years? Heavens! And me? Nothing, never sick, even with a cold washcloth on my throat to try to get my temperature up to a hundred. Are you finished with this farce yet? There's nothing wrong with you at all, she tells me, when I swear, bent over double, that I am about to die standing there on my own feet, that very instant. Nobody understands that with a mother who's been operated on ten times in ten years I've developed a hollow, orphaned illness, whose symptoms I haven't yet been able to define, but that exist, and that's the only thing left to take from me to give my mother.

This time she is dying, I went to live elsewhere and in exchange she's moved away. Every time I move, it sets in motion a reaction, a result that is outside me. I do something, and it affects my mother. When I was inside her, feeling my body move made her dizzy, even though I'm the one whose head was upside down. Now, I'm walking toward her, so there is surely going to be some sort of incident on the way, something will happen to me, or at least an idea will come, after all the time I've been looking for one, to save her and lose myself. I'm walking, and when I get there, she'll have blisters, that's the way it works with us. When I have a belly-ache, they remove her colon; when I have a headache, they find a cyst behind her eye. If I'm hurting somewhere, right away my mother is dying. If I'm afraid, she calls to me; if I'm thirsty, she sweats—you've never seen anyone give so much for so little in return. If I take, she gives. If I walk, she comes running. If I leave, she comes back. There, that's it, I'll try that. It would be great.